"An alien creature was recently captured in Florida," the President of Earth said. "A juvenile. A child, in fact. But high-ranking. Possibly a runaway prince. Comes from a world called Jamborango; has a name that sounds like Qumax. He's wanted back home, and he won't get home if he gets loose and our xenophobic populace gets their hands on him. The alien ship—"

"*You mean we've made contact with an alien civilization?*"

The president looked pained. "Pay attention, Harold. Why do you think I summoned you?"

There was that. Why *would* he summon the Minister of Inner-Galactic Affairs, if not to handle an Inner-Galactic Affair? "Uh . . . Freddie, I . . ."

The most powerful man on Earth sighed. "It's my penalty, I suppose, for installing my deadbeat cousin as head of a pseudo-ministry . . ."

Tor books by Piers Anthony

THE E.S.P. WORM

PIERS ANTHONY AND ROBERT E. MARGROFF

A TOM DOHERTY ASSOCIATES BOOK
NEW YORK

This is a work of fiction. All the characters and events portrayed in this book are fictitious, and any resemblance to real people or events is purely coincidental.

THE E.S.P. WORM

Copyright © 1970 by Robert E. Margroff and Piers Anthony

A Tor Book
Published by Tom Doherty Associates, Inc.
49 West 24th Street
New York, N.Y. 10010

Cover art by Don Maitz

ISBN: 0-812-51916-7

First Tor printing: November 1986

Printed in the United States of America

0 9 8 7 6 5 4 3 2

~~~~~~~ **Chapter 1** ~~~~~~~

I had been smashing planets for half an hour, and my best shot of the day was coming up. I leaned over the sun and took careful aim at Venus, ready to carom it off Mars and score on three planetoids simultaneously.

A brown strand crossed my vision: my annoying, unmanageable hair. I brushed it back impatiently and resumed my stance. I held my breath, began my motion—

BUUUZZZAAAKK! went the communiset. My arm jerked. The cometcue angled away, colliding with a nebula, then a vacuum seal, then the Jupiter sphere and on back into a sunspot where of course it was out of play. Jupiter's moon Ganymede spun out of orbit, up, down, sideways, bufferwards and finally into the "half-gravity" trap.

I eyed the carnage and swore. I banged the comm switch on. "You misbegotten apefaced baggiebusting idiot!" I shouted at my untimely caller. "This is a private line—"

I paused about then. The face in the screen was that of the President of the World.

"Emergency," he snapped. "Get over here immediately, Harold." He seemed preoccupied. Maybe he hadn't heard me.

"Sure, Freddy," I mumbled, somewhat daunted. Sometimes his actions were irritatingly peremptory, but he *was* the chief officer of Earth. He was also my only cousin. Indeed, I owed my present sinecure to him. This was not nepotism so much as convenience—but I never dwelt on that unduly.

"Move!" he yelled. "It's high time you earned your paycheck."

The term "paycheck" was archaic if not obsolete in our credit-balance economy, but I decided not to stand on technicalities. I moved.

I rode the corridor belt past pictures and other strategically placed reminders of past administrations. What could Freddy want with me in such a hurry? True, my door bore the legend MINISTER OF INNER-GALACTIC WORLD AFFAIRS, but that was meaningless. Unless something special had come up. Maybe I should have watched the news this morning. . . .

I glided around a bend, admiring my perfect poise as my belt intersected the belt from a cross-hall—and converged with a starchy baggie-dress. The metallic hoops and bustles of the thing bounced me back like a planetoid from the buffer.

"Why don't you watch where you're—" I began, but had to pause again. The head above the baggie was blonde and so adorably feminine that I regretted never having seen it before. And here I was on the way to the Office, unable to dally!

"Minister Prodkins," she said, her voice like the caress of a clean summer breeze. She held out a gloved hand. "I'm Dr. Dilsmore."

"Just what I've always wanted," I said, squeezing the proffered digit with unseemly intimacy while I wondered who she was and how she knew me. That baggie might conceal a figure with all the sex appeal of a sprouting potato, for all I could see, but somehow I had the impression of buxom youth.

"The extraterrestrialogist," she said, as though that clarified anything.

"That's, uh, very interesting," I mumbled, wishing the baggie would pass before a strong light. The President's sanctum loomed before us, and I knew I had to cut this short. "If you'd like to leave your comm number—" As though a dish like this would give her number to a nothing like me! I stood hardly taller than she, and sported neither muscle nor brain. Apart from my ability at Solar Pool, I was talentless—particularly when it came to women. But I had to try.

"Of course, since we'll be working together," she agreed to my amazement. "But we'd better not keep the President waiting."

Working together! For a tantalizing moment tomcats and billygoats pranced through my romance-starved mind. But that was ridiculous.

Then we were past the guards and lined up like truants before the prune-faced secretary. "You may go right in, Minister Prodkins," she said sourly. "You, Dr. Dilsmore, take a seat—if such a thing is possible in that contraption."

For the first time and probably the last time I felt a flicker of camaraderie with Pruneface. She antedated the baggie-dress, and was not afraid to show her contempt of the style. No lesser person than the President's secretary could afford such an opinion, however; certainly *I* couldn't. Not openly.

But the blonde had to be someone important, to be known by sight here. In fact—

I had no time to ponder further, for President

Frederik Bascum was within his lair. "Sit down, Harold. It's time I had a talk with you."

I sat. This wasn't like the President and it wasn't like the stern, stodgy, but politically brilliant older cousin I'd known. I studied the gray hairs in his elegant mustache, the ice-crevasse lines in his face. I had to admit he was an impressive figure.

"Harold," he said, steepling his hands in that practiced way of his, "it may surprise you to learn that you are about to take an active part in government. Oh, it will be suitably small for you to handle, but don't underrate its importance."

"Naturally not," I murmured, more mystified than ever. Freddy had not spoken to me like this before. In fact, he had seemed happy to keep me entirely out of sight and without responsibility.

"As you know if you have been watching the news analysts, Earth has now made contact with a race that we assume is inner-galactic. You have therefore become an important man."

I looked at him, considering the incredible thing he had uttered. Either he had finally succumbed to the strain of the Office, or I had missed something in the news. Or both. "I suppose you're right, Mr. President."

"Of course I'm right! And knowing your proclivities as I do, I'm sure you're entirely confused right now. You probably spent the morning practicing Solar Pool and dreaming about anachronistic distaff apparel, and never bothered to keep up with world events."

I did not dignify such a crass insinuation with a reply. He had me dead to rights.

"Very well," he said tiredly, "I'll tell you what you need to know. I suppose you can't help being an albatross. It's my penalty for succumbing to a simplistic solution—installing a deadbeat relative in a pseudo-ministry."

He seemed to have summed up that part of it very succinctly. Freddy was a realist.

"An alien creature was recently captured in Florida," he said. "A juvenile. A child, in fact. But high-ranking. Possibly a runaway prince. Comes from a world that sounds to us like Jamborango; has a name that sounds like Qumax. He's wanted back home, and he won't get home if he gets loose and our xenophobic populace spots him. The alien ship—"

"You mean we've made contact with an alien civilization?"

He looked pained. "Please pay attention, Harold. Why do you think I've summoned you?"

There was that. Why *would* he summon the Minister of Inner-Galactic World Affairs, if not to handle an Inner-Galactic Affair?

That reminded me of the blonde in the outer office. If she were part of that Affair . . .

"The alien ship," Freddy resumed determinedly, "we have been in contact with is not really a police craft. That's a cover story we adopted for sundry and sufficient reasons. A ship will land to reclaim this problem child, but it won't be a cruiser. Actually it's more of a cargo ship that Qumax's parent casually ordered off from some adjacent trade line."

"Is this a nonhuman alien?" I inquired, intrigued.

The President pressed a button that elevated a solid-projector to his desk top. A three-dimensional still came on.

"Ulp!" I said, or words to that effect.

Imagine the biggest, ugliest cabbage worm since the dawn of cabbage worms on Earth. Add a bulging cranium and two black shiny antennae. Add

two eyes glinting with the lights of intelligence—
dark eyes, though, like pits into eternity. Move
down on the sausage-shaped body, skipping over
the greasy folds like freshly turned furrows, all the
way back to where the shoulders extend into twin
flesh lumps attached to clusters of brachiating
greenish-gray tentacles. That, plus a long taper
back to a blunt and solid-looking wrinkly tail, was
Qumax.

"You can see now why I summoned you," Freddy
said, shutting off the projector.

"Yes . . ." I began, and found my inspiration
exhausted. I was not much for speechmaking at
great moments. My mock position had abruptly
become real, and I had a job to do that literally
affected the world. Contact with a civilized, galactic, alien species! Why, this could revolutionize
our society!

"We'll have a trebvee actor make some of your
critical public appearances," he was saying, "and
a battery of experts will prepare your statements.
We may not be able to protect you entirely from
the press, but Dr. Dilsmore will run interference
for you and avert complete disaster."

I had known my cousin didn't think much of me,
but the implications hurt. He was so sure I'd bungle it that he was making me a complete figure-
head. And he was saying it right to my face, as
though my thoughts and feelings had no relevance
at all. There were unwritten volumes of contempt
in his attitude—whole libraries of underestimation.

I sat there, nerving myself to prove how wrong
he had been about Harold Prodkins, former black
sheep. I had no intention of being a—

The President activated his comm. "Send in Dr.
Dilsmore, please."

Oops! I didn't want *her* present while I braced Freddy. "Mr. President—" I began.

"Later, Harold. This is important."

That did it. I marshaled my intellectual forces as the blonde entered. Her name, it developed, was Nancy.

"Dr. Dilsmore," Freddy said briskly, "I think it would be best if you gave the Minister an account of your first encounter with the alien Qumax. We don't want Harold to appear ignorant if the press gets at him." There was a slight stress on the word "appear."

"Eh, before you do that, Doctor," I said, "I wonder if you can give me the gist of the seventy-eighth amendment to the World Constitution?"

She looked surprised, but her aplomb did not suffer. "The seventy-eighth? Isn't that the one that puts you in complete charge of all dealings with inner-galactics?"

The President was irritated at the interruption. "A formality. The congress never supposed—"

"It puts the man holding my office in charge," I clarified. "And that man, once appointed by the President, holds office for a similar term and can be removed only by death or impeachment or unsolicited resignation. Do you remember, Doctor, what kind of dealings I'm empowered to handle?"

She looked attractively perplexed. "Why—all kinds. Everything having to do with inner-galactics. Trade treaties, alliances, whatever. You can act without congress and without the President."

"This is ridiculous," Freddy exclaimed. "That amendment was ratified in extreme haste by an outgoing congress who thought, erroneously, that Earth had received a signal from outer space. The press of other business prevented the office from being abolished after the signal's fraudulence was clarified. After that, congressional inertia—"

"But the statute does remain on the books, doesn't it, Mr. President," I said. "And so I have extraordinary powers because that bygone congress, rightly or wrongly, feared that there would not be time for the conventional system, in its glacial haste, to deal effectively with aliens if they appeared suddenly. As it seems they have. So—"

Freddy's face had taken on an asbestos hue. I had surprised him, and he did not much appreciate the experience. "And now, Doctor," I continued blithely, turning back to the female extraterrestrialogist, "suppose you give me that account the President so kindly suggested. Just so the Minister of Inner-Galactic World Affairs won't *appear* ignorant."

"Nearly three days ago," she said without hesitation, "I was taken to a section of Florida swamp where the alien and several persons of low degree had been rendered unconscious by a quantity of Jupegas. Apparently Qumax had been endeavoring to use these people to help him find his way home. That part isn't clear yet."

"Hmmm, yes," I said, stroking my beardless chin. "And exactly what was your impression of this—(I thought of the horrible solid photograph and suppressed a shudder)—child, Doctor?"

"My impression was that Qumax *is* a child. When he woke up surrounded by the might of our planet, he—he cried. He let loose big tears just as a human child might. I couldn't help feeling sorry for him. Any woman would."

"Well, that's understandable, I suppose," I said uncomfortably. Sorry for *that?* I'd as soon step on it! "How does this tie in with the alien ship?"

"Qumax knew our language. When he contacted

his—well, the translation seems to be Swarm Tyrant, or perhaps Harem Sheik—I think he was genuinely frightened. This Swarm Tyrant's image was a bit hazy, coming as it did from goodness knows how far. Maybe the set wasn't working properly. I admit the creature did terrify *me*, at least, and I'm not a child."

It occurred to me that before the baggie style came into fashion, women had not needed to say whether they were children. Visible anatomy had made their status plain.

"But when the child—when Qumax—learned that the Tyrant was angry at Earth, not him, his manner changed completely. He demanded VIP treatment: his own trebvee set, gadgets from his spacecraft, special food not mentioned by the Tyrant ... in fact, he's had everything his own way except that he's caged."

"I suppose that's Lucifernia—the maximum security prison?"

"Protective custody," Freddy said quickly.

"And this Swarm Sheik went overboard?"

"He certainly didn't apologize for our inconvenience! He gave us to understand that he wanted—demanded!—us to take good care of his—his larva—and he hinted that he would be most displeased if he found anything out of order. A serious infraction on our part might lead him to snuff out our sun, he said ... and I don't think he was bluffing. Qumax put me in mind of an undisciplined brat, and that Tyrant was just plain insufferable."

"Then he will have to apologize," I said. "He will have to apologize handsomely to Earth—and maybe we'll demand more than mere words!"

The President of the World lost his bedraggled composure. He made a sound evidently preliminary to a categorical denial. In fact, he choked.

"Mr. Minister," said Dr. Nancy Dilsmore excitedly, her hair flouncing with the vigor of her nodding. "Mr. Minister, I agree completely!"

At twelve noon the longtime leftover election signs along the automated highway presented an uninspiring view. DO YOU WANT YOUR DAUGHTER TO BE A HARLOT? screamed one, showing the noble face of the now World President—Freddy—in his stern Moses-with-Commandments profile. HELP ELECT THE DECENT PEOPLE'S CHOICE pleaded a second. HELP STAMP OUT PORNOGRAPHIC DRESS urged a third. A fourth proclaimed FREDERIK MICHAEL BASCUM FOR WORLD PRESIDENT, and had a portrait of Freddy smiling approvingly at a bag in a baggie dress. I found it sickening. But those slogans had swept Freddy to victory in four continents. Whether he had led the world into the apex of New Victorianism or merely ridden NV into power, both man and attitude were now disgustingly entrenched.

The good-looking Ph.D (from the top of her head to the bottom of her—head) was sad evidence of that. Her baggie bulged outward as she sat, like the folds of a broken accordion, providing her torso with all the lithe luster of a pregnant marsupial frog recently trodden on. She probably slept in that bag, so that at no hour of the day or night would any hint of any untoward (i.e., feminine) anatomy be manifest. I longed for a return of the fashions of the past century, when bosoms had been only nominally covered, and shapes had been shaped. Today, even in the best libraries, certain pages of the history texts had been blacked out. Those old-time fashions had been deemed indecent, you see. Some expensive boot-leggers carried unexpurgated copies, but possession was a ticket to rehabilitation at places like Lucifernia. Alas, I had been born too late, and probably never would see a live female torso. Even household pets wore fluffy clothing these days, and babies were diapered in darkness.

Lucifernia loomed on the horizon like a bad-tempered thundercloud, grim warning to lascivious thinkers like me. "It's even worse inside," Nancy Dilsmore said, mistaking my expression. "That poor innocent little alien, shut away deep underground."

"I thought it was a spoiled brat."

"It's still a child," she pointed out, and I let the matter be. The truth was, I found her feminine illogic rather appealing.

All too soon we arrived at the massy twin gates of the goblin mountain and were gulped inside. Our air cushion hardly disturbed the light gray dust on the prison roadway. We passed electrified barbed wire emplacements and tall lookout towers snouted with large caliber machine guns and squat grenade launchers. Beyond these were ballistic missile sites and nozzles for nerve gas and flamethrowers. Then the sleek male tanks and sleeker female jet fighters. And several heavy-duty laser units. And I suspected a minefield or two, and maybe a battleship; there was a large enough moat, anyway, with signs proclaiming DANGER—ACID and UNSAFE—RADIATION and even TIGER CROSSING. None of them were intended to be funny.

I was beginning to feel sympathy for that alien child.

We parked at last and the automatic controls died. Two automations in human guise stomped up. We were escorted through a portcullis into a metal antechamber where we were frisked by X-ray. A technician whistled and Nancy blushed, making me madder than ever at that baggie dress. There had to be real goodies concealed beneath those opaque hoops!

But we were being hustled into an inner chamber. An elevator, in fact, for as the doors ground closed behind us, isolating us, the descent began.

There was hardly room for Nancy's baggie and me. I felt like grabbing the thing and ripping it apart. Who knew—she might be nude thereunder!

She looked about nervously, as though divining my concupiscent imaginings. "Mr. Minister, this isn't—"

"Harold," I hinted.

She collapsed against me with a little sigh. The ribs of the baggie dug into my natural ones. I stumbled back against the wall, my hands searching for some place to catch hold of her under the tent before she fell to the floor. My fingers punched through the taunt material and groped across mind-expanding surfaces.

Nancy was not being affectionate, unfortunately. She was unconscious.

H-i-s-s-s-s-t! I felt something sting my left shoulder and knew it immediately for an invisible splinter of frozen Jupegas, that all-purpose anesthetic. Of all the times to be hit! I thought with despairing frustration.

And passed out myself.

~~~~~ Chapter 2 ~~~~~

My head was itching. It was as though a monstrous mosquito had lodged its iron proboscis within my skull and sucked out twenty cc of my gray matter, depositing a similar quantity of irritant.

I woke up in a foul temper, unable to scratch at the agony, because my cranium got in the way. My eyes moved, left to right, up and down. Wherever they turned green blanketing appeared. Four walls, a ceiling and a floor—all padded. Light filtered through from a recessed ventilator.

It looked as though I had finally come to the end my relatives had direly predicted. I was wearing gray prison coveralls and soft slippers, and my brain hurt. I couldn't care less what the doctors said about the brain having no pain receptors; it *hurt*. Probably courtesy of the Jupegas dose, though I had always understood that the anesthetic from our giant brother planet was completely free of aftereffects. Some things have to be learned the hard way.

But why? Why was I here in this cell? I was no criminal. I was Earth's Minister of Inner-Galactic World Affairs, and I had come to inspect a loathsome captive alien creature. Along with a luscious lady Ph.D. And what had they done with Nancy?

I tried to work up a righteous fury, but the incessant itch in my head dissipated the necessary concentration. I refused, at any rate, to throw a tantrum. I was sure I was being watched.

A padded section pushed open and I recognized a door. Behind it was a cubicle, and within that space was a soft plastic tray loaded with food. Coffee, fried eggs, nicely browned ham, a stack of golden wheatcakes and a thimble of bright maple syrup.

I realized I was ravenous. I grabbed the tiny rubber spoon and fell to. In a moment I discarded the utensil, since it tended to bend rather than cut, and crammed the morsels into my mouth with my fingers. I ate everything. I licked the last drop of coffee from the cup, ran my tongue over the hotcake plate, inspected my sleeves for suckable syrup stains.

After everything was more than gone, I realized that I had never been that kind of a pig before. And I was still hungry.

There was a tiny toilet in one corner, really no more than a padded hole in the floor, and a low-pressure rubber faucet. No mirror, no towel, no soap and certainly no razor. I cleaned up as well as I could, glad that the awful itch had finally subsided.

After about an hour—my watch was gone, naturally—another door cranked open, and two of the slab-faced guards took me away. We passed through interminable tunnels and alleys and up ramps and by cloisters and finally debouched into a plush office.

Nancy was there.

Her honey-blonde hair now hung to shoulder-length, and her shoulders . . . showed. Her baggie was gone, replaced by coveralls similar to mine, except for the bulges. I had not observed rondure like that since my last furtive look at a porno photograph: *Woman In Street Clothes, Circa 1990*. I tried to keep my eyes from bulging lasciviously, not to mention certain other anatomy.

"Much better than baggies, aren't they," a harsh male voice said. I jumped guiltily. It was—I recognized his porcine profile—the infamous warden of Lucifernia. Something-or-other Nitti. I did not like him.

Nancy turned her blue eyes on me, but did not speak. I saw with a shock that her hands, all the way up to the wrists, were naked. Some of her forearm even showed where the sleeve hung loosely.

"I thought you two would like to watch a trebcast," Nitti said, burbling with some obnoxious humor. One wall illuminated as he spoke: a ten-by-ten foot receiving screen. The guards shoved me into a chair facing it. What was going on?

The dateline flashed, and I had another shock. A full day had passed! No wonder I had been hungry. I had been knocked out by the Jupegas, or whatever else they might have given me later, for a good twenty hours.

In the screen appeared a view that was three dimensional, for a trebvee receiver had depth as well as area. It was the broadcasting studio of one of Earth's most distinguished newsmen: Alvin Swept. He glanced at the worldwide audience with that penetrating demeanor that compelled instant attention, whether he was breaking a major news

scoop or telling a joke. He had always impressed
me as an intelligent, sincere man.

"Tonight," said Alvin Swept, "I am honored to
act as moderator at a very special interview with
Earth's Minister of Inner-Galactic World Affairs,
the honorable Harold W. Prodkins. With him is
the noted Extraterrestrialogist Dr. Nancy Dilsmore.
Participating with me on this panel will be—"

I didn't hear the rest of the build-up. This thing
was impossible! I wasn't on any trebcast, and neither was Nancy. Unless—

Unless there was a trebvee pickup on us now,
and we were about to be interviewed by remote
control.

Awful! I ran my hand over my stubbled chin and
touched my disheveled hair. I looked at the linger-
ing syrup stain on my sleeve. And what would I
say! I knew almost nothing of the situation. And
Nancy—it would wipe her out, socially, if she were
exhibited before the world in that calamitously
exposive prison outfit. Her neck down to the very
collarbone, her hands, her ankles all showing bra-
zenly, and the sensual contours of her torso bur-
geoning under the scant cloth . . .

In the screen appeared a shot of the Capitol
House while the World Anthem blasted dismally.
Then—

Minister Harold Prodkins and scientist Nancy
Dilsmore. Both apparently garbed—the one in a
conservative but handsome suit, the other in an
ornate but fully decorous baggie.

Doubles! I should have remembered Freddy's
threat to use them. Of course! I had proved to be
obstreperous, so my model-of-integrity cousin had
expediently had me incarcerated while he made
other arrangements. And Nancy too, since she had
been so shortsighted as to agree with my position,

and to stand up for the dignity of Earth. We were out of it.

All my posturing had been for nothing. Freddy had shut up and used his brain. If I had used *my* brain, feeble as it was compared to his, I would have known this would happen. Smart, smart Harold Prodkins, who should have stuck to Solar Pool and not attempted to interfere with his cousin's politics.

"Minister Prodkins," Alvin Swept inquired with just the proper tinge of respect, "is it true that Earth has at last made contact with an Inner-Galactic species?"

My double didn't bat his phony eye. "Perfectly true, Alvin. As you newsmen have been very much aware, contact was accomplished secretly soon after the alien landed—crash-landed, actually—in Florida, in the old region of America."

Now the real questioning began, and I had to admit my double was sharp. He had my mannerisms down almost perfectly, and he hesitated in just the right places. "The names would mean nothing," he was saying in reply to a query about the exact identity of the alien creature. "The world sounds like Jamborango (a slight stumble over the pronunciation, just as I would have stumbled) so that's what we're calling it. Jamborango (more confidence)—somewhere near the center of the galaxy. Well out of our present technological reach."

And, cleverly, in reply to preplanned questions (probably the entire interview had been rehearsed and taped and edited hours ago), the whole story came out. All except the real truth: that I had asserted Earth's right to an apology from an insufferable Swarm Tyrant, and had intended to demand it, regardless of Freddy's caution. And Dr. Dilsmore had agreed with me.

Freddy was pulling it off, though. Those doubles, properly bolstered by rigged interviews, could pacify world curiosity until the alien worm Qumax was safely offplanet. Then—

I looked at Nancy and tried to smile reassuringly. She smiled back, despite her dishabille. But both efforts were weak.

For how could Freddy ever allow us to go free to spread the truth? That would destroy his career. It was quite possible that we both faced unofficial life sentences in Lucifernia.

Or worse.

"There," said Warden Nitti as the program concluded, "you have it. So—"

Then an odd look came over him. He made as if to scratch his head, stopped, started to stand up, began to sweat, and finally plumped down again. He seemed to be suffering a siege of the most intense internal strife. Hate and doubt and fear all warred upon his features. Then the face and body calmed, and he turned to the nearest guard. "Your gun, please—hand it over!"

Suddenly I was all-the-way scared. Nitti was about to take the initiative and liquidate us on the spot!

The guard drew his Jupegas gun and handed it to Nitti, who put his fat finger on the trigger and raised the pinched nozzle. I watched the coil-barrel rotate. . . .

"Harold!" Nancy cried.

That got me moving. I lurched to my feet and dove for the warden. There was a sinister hiss as the gun fired, and a blast of icy air struck my ear. But the sliver of Jupeice had missed. I barreled into Nitti, grabbing for his gun-hand. He was far heavier and stronger than I, but I had to make the attempt before he put me away.

His other hand came up heavily and caught my uniform. As I wrestled for the gun, I felt the fabric tearing. Of course prison clothing tore readily, so that it could not be used for strangulations or hand-over-hand descents from cell windows—but this was embarrassing. He had hooked his fingers into the collar of the prison unionsuit—all that I wore beneath the coveralls—and as his meaty arm jerked down all of it ripped away.

I got the gun by grabbing it with both hands and twisting hard. Then I wrestled my way clear of Nitti, leaving my clothing with him. I aimed at his ample torso and fired. The gun cooled in my hand. Frost formed on the snout, and the warden passed out. I shucked out of the sleeves and pantlegs, since they were attached to nothing now.

Nancy was struggling with the armed guard. Suddenly he leaped into the air, did a flipflop, and came down heavily beside the warden. The other guard was already unconscious: the first Jupegas sliver Nitti had fired had struck him.

We ran. There was no chance to escape Lucifernia and we both knew it, but we had to try. I held the gun and led the way.

Suddenly the itch was back in my skull, ferociously. But I didn't—couldn't—stop. "The keys!" I shouted. And dashed back into the warden's office.

The one guard who hadn't been Juped was climbing to his feet. I put him away without even considering the matter. I hauled at Nitti's body, searching for his set of master keys. My hands seemed to know what they were doing better than I did. In a moment I had them: a dozen colored bars mounted on a large ring.

The itch was tearing my head apart! I charged out again, past Nancy, and ran down the hall. At the end was an elevator. I rammed a key into the key-slot, and the door opened. Phenomenal luck, that I should hit the right one without even looking! I pulled Nancy in with me and punched for the basement.

As the unit slid smoothly downward the itch abated and I remembered that I was naked except for my slippers and a forgotten shred of sleeve.

I tried to hide behind the keys, but Nancy didn't say anything.

Then I saw that she had suffered some battle-erosion herself. There was a long tear down the side of her coveralls, exposing her flesh from bra to panty. (I didn't like using such filthy words, even in my mind, in connection with a decent woman—but I knew no other terms to describe her underclothing.) I felt sorry for her. Probably no man had seen that flesh before except the doctor who delivered her as a baby. Now it was open to the vulgar gaze of a comparative stranger.

That reminded me just how insidiously New Victorianism had developed. Twenty years ago the ankle-length skirts and wrist-length sleeves had seemed like a transitory fashion—but somehow it had transited into even greater repression, not into physical enlightenment. If only someone had cried "foul!" while there was still time, before an entire generation had been brainwashed. Now we had Freddy and the baggie.

Well, the damage was done, I thought as I took another look in Nancy's suit. I had compromised her; I would have to marry her. If I survived this misadventure, and if she did.

The elevator stopped, unfortunately. The itch struck again. I shoved open the door.

It opened to a solid rock. Undaunted, I touched the stone, my fingers pressing nimbly at certain points in precise combination.

CLICK! Pause. I touched another section. "To deprime the bomb," I explained. CLICK! And the stone slid aside.

I hauled Nancy after me as I ran down the dank passage that was revealed, lurched around a corner, fingered another section of the wall, and stepped into the new passage that yawned open. Warm air blasted out and struck my body. We charged down the unlit hallway, and behind us the stone slammed back into place. My head was splitting.

Yet another turn—and yet another door—and then we stood at the brink of a large pit. Its floor was flat, and covered by a rug. There was a large trebvee set and elegant furniture.

My head suddenly clear, I peered down at the biggest, ghastliest cabbage worm I had ever seen photographed. Writhing octopus clusters, lipless green mouth, convex eyelids closing like window-shades, breath smelling of licorice. . . .

"Hi ya, Rubes!" Qumax said.

~~~~~ Chapter 3 ~~~~~

NANCY exercised her female prerogative to get
the first word in. Her voice only a little strained,
she said, "Happy Jack Bumperty, I presume?"

The green monster blinked. "Happy Jack is a
trebvee clown."

"So he is. Your impression was perfect."

Qumax's head twisted to one side. Green skin
rippled from his neckless head (or maybe his headless neck) to his blunt tail—about twelve linear
feet of twitch. His frog-mouth opened and produced a sound like live steam escaping through
dead peanut husks.

Nancy shuddered. "Qumax, I don't think I'll ever
get used to the way you laugh."

"You don't need to," Qumax said. "Humans never
need to. Hearing me laugh is a rare privilege."

"Qumax, you're still trying to get inside my brain.
That's a gross violation of privacy."

I had been waiting for an opportunity to break
in, but this made me pause. Was Qumax a mind
reader?

26

My head itched again. "More than that, Rube," Qumax said. "Hey, Nancy—you know what this creep thought when he saw into your coveralls? He felt real masculine all of a sudden, and—"

"Qumax!" she snapped severely.

The reprimand set the worm back only momentarily. "But I'd really like to know what *you* thought, when he shucked his suit and dragged you away—"

"I knew you were in control, Qumax. You took over the warden and made him shoot one guard—"

"Would have been *both* guards, if hotshot here hadn't interfered," the worm said sullenly. "So I had to take him over, before he messed things up any more. Would have been easier if I could have worked through you, though, sweetheart. You really shouldn't have taken that Yoga training to gain complete mind and body control."

"Mental privacy is even more important than physical, Qumax. When you learn that, you won't be such a child."

The worm's body had slithered forward during this interchange, and the process fascinated me. Well, slither isn't the proper word. Rumple, maybe. His torso touched the floor in two or three places, and those places stayed firm while the vertical loops somehow traveled forward. I had seen something like that in films of a sidewinder rattlesnake once, but never did understand how it worked.

The creature was close under us now, head about level with our feet. A tentacle reached up toward Nancy. "A Jam child is far more mature than a human adult," Qumax said.

Suddenly the itch exploded in my head. My right hand swung out and clapped Nancy hard across the resilient buttocks.

"Oh!" she cried—and tumbled into the pit.

Qumax made a gleeful frying sound, twisting his

gross loops about in a paroxysm of mirth. Adult, hell! I thought. A brat in any shape was still a brat.

Nancy landed lithely—the fall had only been about five feet—and back away from the alien. But the exertion had ripped her uniform further. I gasped at the sight of more female flesh than I had, literally, ever dreamed about. (How can you dream when you have no model to work from?) Even married couples were supposed to use a tall bundling board and keep the lights out when going about the sordid necessities leading to propagation of the species.

Then the itch had hold of me once more, and I jumped down after her. I tried to fight it, realizing that Qumax was controlling my body—as he had been doing every time my head hurt, except maybe at the beginning—but was unable to help myself. I ran forward and grabbed for her.

Nancy turned, put up her arms (and dazzled me through the gaping clothing) and caught hold of mine. I found myself flying through the air and then falling flat on the carpeting.

"That hurt!" Qumax cried, and I realized that while he controlled my body, he also absorbed my sensations. It had to be that way, or he would be operating blindly. I felt the abrasion of elbows and knees only dimly through the itch; the worm had taken the brunt of pain.

"You knew I was trained for this," Nancy shot back. "Why don't you just admit you can't control me and—"

"HISSSS," said Qumax, sounding like a flattening truck tire. Impelled by the itch I got up and attempted a football tackle on Nancy. This time I landed on my nose, and knew that I would have done better if I'd had control of my own muscles.

"SSSSS!" Qumax sounded as I fell. Yes, it hurt him. Then suddenly he wasn't in my head, and I was able to look up at Nancy and force a smile at her.

"I don't like to cause pain to anyone or anything," she said, pulling her suit together. "Qumax, if you persist—"

She paused, as though rebuffing another mental siege.

Then the itch was back and I was making another lunge. This time I got her: I clamped my arms around her small waist, locked one hand over one wrist, and grabbed at her coveralls with the other hand. I was behind her, my hands in front. My palm pressed against—

Then the mind presence was gone again, and I felt her stiffen. Qumax was attacking her again, and there I was hanging on to her . . . chest. The giant worm rumpled up, and the massed tentacles were reaching for both of us.

I hurled Nancy sidewise and shouldered into Qumax. His writhing digits touched me repulsively, but my weight was enough to rock back his forepart. He lost his balance and fell, his tail slapping frantically at the rug. The worm-shape was not ideal on a flat surface.

I ran to Nancy to help her up. She was unconscious. Had she banged her head when I threw her down? I had only done it to save her from the alien!

Qumax righted himself. "Stupid female," he complained. "She fainted when you squeezed her boob. Prudish mammal!"

"I never—" But of course I *had*. My hand still tingled with the memory. Qumax had made me do it, but full sensation had returned to me when he went after her.

I felt faint myself. This went far beyond mere pornography. That was vicarious. To actually perform such an obscene act—

"The fuzz'll be on our necks in a moment," Qumax said. It was amazing how much old-fashioned slang he had picked up from three days of trebvee. The fuzz on his neck? He didn't even have a neck, unless it was his entire body. "I'll just have to make do with you, I guess. She has a much better mind, but I can't get at it. Not in the time we have. But we'd better bring her along."

"Bring her—" I started, confused. "Where are we going?" I did recognize the need to escape, whatever our personal differences. None of us had much of a future in Lucifernia. Not after the trouble we had caused. Not with Freddy's machinations.

At Qumax's mental spur I picked up Nancy's unconscious form and hoisted it out of the pit. Then I gave Qumax a boost—or rather, I braced myself while he crawled over me. He was astonishingly heavy. No wonder a five-foot wall had been enough to confine him. With no place for him to get a proper tentacle-hold, and the furniture bolted down (and no doubt securely riveted) in the center, he had been helpless. Except for his ability to control human minds. Why hadn't he used that before?

"Because I didn't think of it," he admitted candidly. He was, after all, a child; his experience was limited. "Anyway, there were no good subjects in this hole, and it wasn't time yet."

Time? Oh, the space ship that was coming for him. I hadn't realized it was arriving so soon.

"It isn't the one they expect," he said. "This one happened to be closer, so stopped by to help. My Swarm Tyrant doesn't know about it either. He'll be real mad when his ship comes and Earth can't turn me over!" Again the frying sound.

Somehow I did not share his glee. That Tyrant might very well liquidate our sun, or whatever it was he had threatened. And how did Qumax himself know about that nearer ship?

Before I could consider such things further, Qumax was up, and I had to climb out myself and pick up Nancy again. I wasn't used to such exercise, and she was no light pool cue. But it was either cooperate or feel the itch, and I preferred the former.

We made our way along the various halls and tunnels to the elevator, and piled inside. Qumax's bulk made it uncomfortably crowded. I thought I'd gag on that licorice aroma. We started up.

Nancy's blue eyes opened. "What? What?" she inquired.

"We're, ah, leaving Lucifernia," I said. It was my voice and my statement, but not my conviction. Qumax was out of my head.

Her hand went to her . . . chest. "Harold, what happened after—after—?"

"Nothing," I said. "The worm and I had a discussion and decided to break out. That's all."

"This is suicidal!" she exclaimed, coming fully awake. "We can't just walk out!"

"Why not!" Qumax demanded.

"A disheveled woman, an alien creature, and a naked man?"

Oops! I had forgotten that last.

And then the elevator was gentling to a stop. Qumax pressed a button and the doors slid aside.

There, as I had feared, was the firing squad. Six guards and Nitti.

"Now, my little menagerie," the warden said, "let's have a little chat. About an attempted jailbreak, and an unprovoked attack on duly constituted authorities, and . . . ''

He spun off a whole paragraph of technicalities, but I didn't listen. He must have been dosed with an antidote to the Jupegas, for he obviously hadn't slept for any twenty hours. His suit was rumpled where I had grabbed him, and he did not seem to be in a good humor.

Seven men, counting Nitti. How many could Qumax control simultaneously? I wished the worm had been paying attention to what lay ahead; he could have landed at another floor. But a brat wouldn't have such elementary foresight.

I peered quickly at my Jamborang cohort and saw the reaction I had been half expecting. Qumax was quivering in dismay. Obviously, if he could control more than one person at a time, he would have hung on to me while attacking Nancy. Instead, he had tackled us one at a time.

"The warden!" Nancy stage-whispered, poking Qumax just beneath the cluster of tentacles. "He gives the orders—"

"No talking in the ranks!" Nitti barked. "I'm in charge here, and—and I say—" His expression grew even uglier than usual. "I say—" Fear came and went. "I say—" He formed a greasy smile. "I say we'll take my personal copter. March!"

Had Qumax succeeded in taking over? I wasn't sure. But I knew Nitti had a skull-sized itch along about now.

At any rate, we marched. A woman, a worm, and a naked man. Down the hall, through an office, out a door, into a courtyard open to the sky.

A sentry came to life. "Halt!" he cried. "Show your passes."

"I'm taking these prisoners to my copter," Nitti said.

"By what authority?"

"By my own authority! I'm the warden."

"The Jamborangan entity is confined according to the directive of the President of the World. Show me his authorization."

Oh-oh. Divided authority here. Trouble.

The sentry made the peculiar combination of faces, and I knew that the itch had transferred itself to his head. "Very well. Pass," he said at last.

But if Qumax had transferred control to the sentry, what about Nitti?

"Jailbreak! Jailbreak!" Nitti cried suddenly. "Oh, my parboiled head! Gas them all!"

Qumax had bungled it. For now Nitti knew the score.

The men milled about in confusion, not comprehending this abrupt change. Nancy reached over, grabbed a Jupegas gun, and pulled the trigger. Slivers of ice shot out in a steady stream. She swung the weapon in a half circle before us, and suddenly we three were the only ones standing.

It occurred to me that I wouldn't like to have this woman mad at me.

After that it was almost routine. Qumax summoned an attendant, made him show us where the copter was, made him phone down instructions to let the warden's aircraft pass, and then had me gas the attendant with one of the other guns. We climbed into the machine.

"Now," Nancy said, "we have only three problems."

"We don't have time for a discussion," I said nervously. "We have to get out of here before they discover what we've done and activate the defenses." The thought of those defenses chilled me. I hardly cared to be goosed by a missile.

"That's the first problem," she said. "Which of us knows how to fly a military copter?"

I looked at Qumax and he looked at me. Blanks.

"Next problem," she said, brisk as a school-teacher. "Which of us knows the safe route past the airborne minefields and the territory covered by the automatic antiaircraft emplacements?"

Blanks.

"And just how long will it be before they find Nitti and give him the antidote again? Long enough for us to blunder out of his vengeful, all-points-bulletin reach?"

"I'm only a misunderstood alien child," Qumax said, and began to cry.

Nancy rolled her eyes skyward. "Well, we're committed now. We'll all be crucified if we stay here. Harold, you go drag the warden to the copter. He'll be able to fly us out safely, and that'll keep him out of mischief, too."

Qumax brightened. "Why didn't *I* think of that?"

"Because you're only a misunderstood alien child," she snapped. "See if you can find the Jupegas antidote. We'll need him conscious."

Meekly, Qumax got busy. So did I.

Nitti was heavy. He must have had decades of rich dining at the taxpayers' expense. But somehow I hauled his carcass to the copter, where Nancy gave him a shot of the antidote—Saturngas—that Qumax had found in the machine's first-aid kit. Then Qumax took over his mind and Nitti piloted us slowly and circuitously upward.

Qumax stretched across three let-down passenger seats. I found a civilian suit and made myself halfway presentable. Nancy procured needle and thread and did the same.

Gradually the prison became a dark fearsome shadow with its walls studded with radar antennae and rocket launchers. Overhead, sunlight streamed strong and free. Nitti answered three challenges with three separate passwords and a flash of his badge, and we were not fired on.

"Good thing I'm a Jam," Qumax remarked. "Most galactics can read minds, but can't control actions. They'd be helpless now."

I decided not to comment on how helpless he had seemed before Nancy organized our little escapade.

At last we passed out of Lucifernia. We were free.

The phone rang.

We all jumped. Qumax's rumple landed him on the floor between seats, and he was hard put to it to climb back up. Nancy was first to recover.

"It's the warden's phone," she pointed out. "He should answer it. He can put the copter on automatic now."

Nitti, under mental duress, did just that. He set the controls and pressed the "receive" stud on the control panel. "Warden Nitti speaking."

Freddy's face appeared in the front screen. "Warden, I gave you strict orders to keep that worm confined until the alien ship—"

Then he spied the rest of us. "All right, Harold— what are you up to?"

Before I could answer, Qumax cut in. "Help! Help! Mr. President, this awful man is wormnapping me! He says he—he'll kill me if you try to stop him. Please, please save me from him!"

I opened my mouth to protest, but Nancy kicked me. Then I realized that Qumax was actually putting me in charge, while he continued to control Nitti. I nodded, surreptitiously massaging my bruised ankle. "You'll have to—to pay a big ransom, if you want him back in one segment," I growled. "You know what his Swarm Tyrant will do to Earth if anything happens to him."

"Warden, arrest this man!" Freddy cried.

"Arrest him yourself, Rube," Nitti's voice said. "I'm with Harold."

"And don't send any planes after us," I said. "I mean business. Ten million in small bills. I'll give you twenty-four hours to deliver." But I wondered how he could deliver, if we were avoiding him.

"Do as he says, sir!" Qumax cried pitifully. "He's a bad man!"

"Ridiculous," Freddy said, but he looked uncertain.

"Harold," Nancy whispered urgently. "I—I think we're being followed already."

I glanced at her white face, then followed her quivering finger to the red light rising behind us. Another copter—a large one! Trust Freddy not to communicate until he had the power to back it up.

"Get rid of it," I told Freddy. "Or I'll—"

I hesitated. What would I do, in my assumed capacity as abductor of the alien worm? I saw the blunt tip of Qumax's tail and had a dull inspiration.

I grabbed the tail and hauled it up into the field of view of the phone pickup. The thing was as lumpy and limp as a bean cushion, and sandpaper rough. No wonder Qumax seldom skidded! "I'll start torturing him!" I said with what I hoped was the proper note of fanaticism. I made a face and tweaked the tail gently.

"Ouch! Oooo, that smarts!" Qumax screamed obligingly. He was hamming it up too much, but Freddy seemed impressed. "This monster is killing me! Please, please, Mr. President, do as he says!"

"Harold wouldn't hurt a fly, much less a worm," Freddy said disgustedly.

So much for bluffing. My practical cousin knew me too well. The copter behind gained.

"Take us into those clouds," Nancy said, speaking to Qumax. "And cut off President Bascum—he's using the phone to keep tabs on us."

How nice to have someone smart along, I thought. Nitti's hand flicked the phone switch off and banked the copter to the left. Sure enough, there was a floating mountain of cloud, with outlying islands and a dense interior mass. We shot into that complex, and it was like peasoup fog. Cotton candy that became vapor drifted across our windshield. I hoped nothing solid was hidden there.

I breathed silent relief as the copter began to drop. If we landed under cover of this fog, Freddy's pursuit copter would never find us. Of course we could not exactly pose as tourist civilians—not with Qumax along. We'd have to hide him, scrounge for food, discourage inquiries, wait for his rescueship to arrive. . . .

The wheels touched ground moments after the fog lifted. Rather, I corrected myself, we had come out of the bottom of the cloud, submerging into daylight. Now to conceal the copter and ourselves—

School children came from behind trees to stare. There were eight little country boys in overalls and flannel shirts, and one little girl in a proper baggie and sunbonnet. They gaped at the machine for a while, while we remained frozen with dismay, and then two of the boys tried to boost a third to our canopy. He made it and the brown eyes in the freckled face all but popped out of his head. I could not hear him, but I could imagine what descriptions of Nancy and Qumax his moving mouth was making.

Qumax fried merrily and waved his tentacles at the lad.

I wondered how many minutes it would take for the word to get back to Freddy's minions. The cover had been blown, and we were right back in trouble. Why couldn't the worm for once have acted with discretion—played dead, or hidden under a seat, or something? Did he *want* to be recaptured?

I looked at Nancy. She looked at me. We shrugged fatalistically. Qumax was a child, after all.

Chapter 4

SUDDENLY Nancy remembered what she was wearing. "Well, now you've done it, haven't you, Qumax?" she exclaimed, turning a flaming face on him. "It isn't enough that you disgraced me before Harold and those terrible prison guards! Oh no, you had to let me be seen by children! Goodness knows what this will do to them! You—you should be ashamed of yourself!"

I had thought she was adjusting nicely to the situation, and this surprised me. Maybe she had been too busy to be shy until now, but had suffered a letdown. Or maybe there was something particularly shocking about perverting the tender gaze of children. But most likely she was really angry that Qumax should throw away the escape we had managed, and was berating him on something minor just to let off steam.

"It's you who should be ashamed," Qumax said. "Not for the reasons you imagine, either. But cheer up, it's more than just young humans who will see you. Here comes—"

"Oh no!" Nancy said, and shrank pitifully. When she let down, she really let down. Well, she had performed marvelously until this point, and Qumax had nullified it all, so I could hardly blame her. Why keep fighting, when everything was already lost?

Qumax continued to fry. "Don't worry. There's a lot more hidden. Only the outlines are prominent—"

I forced myself to look sternly at him, much as I had been appreciating those feminine outlines he referred to. "Qumax, Nancy is right. You *should* be ashamed." I was listening for the wail of a police siren, for surely the spectators had given the word by this time. No point in scrambling any more.

I turned to Nancy. "Look, it's only coveralls," I said, still trying not to ogle them. "It's only your hands that are uncovered and if you put them in your pockets—"

Nitti turned around, grinning lasciviously. "Look at those bumps!"

I picked up a gun and let him have a sliver right in the chest. He collapsed, still smiling, and I looked at my hand in shock. I had never been *that* short-tempered before.

"They're nice bumps," I said, trying to cover over the insult and failing dismally. "If it were the custom to show them completely, I'd—I'd *approve* of it!"

You'd go mad with desire, something said in my head. I jumped, then shook it off; I was hallucinating. I was reacting just as ridiculously as she was. It would almost be a relief when the police finally came.

"Oh, Harold, you don't know what it's like," she was saying. "Leered at—by children!"

"It's not your fault," I started comfortingly, already heartily sick of this dialogue. But while I

spoke, Qumax was lowering the ramp and getting
the door open. The door swung upon three elderly
females in very proper bag-dresses. There was no
way they could have avoided seeing the shocking
sight within the copter—a tousled man, an unconscious official, an unbagged woman and a monster
worm. Three elderly breaths sucked sharply in-
wards in unison.

"Well, I never!" said the modern with an obviously black-dyed hair bun.

"Heavens!" said the tight-collared, earmuffed
conservative.

"What is the world coming to!" said the liberal
with high lace collar *and* red-dyed hair bun.

"Ladies, ladies," I said, unstrapping myself from
the seat. I could not remember anchoring myself
for the landing and hadn't been aware of the re-
straint until this moment. I rose and stepped forward, head itching. "We are but three lonely
travelers in search of succor. I and this lovely lady,
and this most significant of aliens—"

"See here," said the conservative. "I'm the Reverend Abigail Swartz and this is the Church of
the Wood's annual Sunday School picnic!"

I quailed behind my worm-sponsored facade. Better to have fallen into a vat of vipers! No group
supported Freddy more devoutly than the collected
Churches of the Wood.

"I'm sure it is," I said. I walked boldly out onto
the ramp and faced them in a manner quite unlike
myself. "Providence has been kind to us." I turned
to Qumax. "Brother Qumax, did you hear what
this magnificent woman has said? This is a Sunday School!" Doom.

"Joy and Hallelujah!" he replied.

"Are you a—a minister?" the reverend asked.

"Fully ordained," I lied. "I am in fact a missionary."

A bewildered expression swept over Abigail's hatchet face. With new horror I realized that my itch was temporarily absent. "Why I do believe—why of course! You are Dr. Andra Moxie, evangelist. Now you've returned to Earth and—it's the strangest thing"—awe timbred her voice—"something whispers to me that you are to redeem us."

"I don't understand," said the modern, her hands to her face. And then she very obviously did. "Yes—I remember now!" She smiled and kept on smiling, despite the agony it must have been.

"Well," said the liberal, "I think"—emotions fought on her face—"that it is truly a great honor you have done us in coming here!"

As though of one mind the three swept forward. I found myself suddenly enveloped by three pairs of well-padded arms. It was an intimacy I could have lived without. Three of the old dears had bad cases of halitosis. And one and all thought it necessary to apply their withered lips to my holy cheek.

It occurred to me that they could not, subconsciously, have been completely unwilling. Otherwise Qumax could never have made three act at once. Unless the rationalization he had proffered through my lips overrode all else, even common sense.

"Ladies," my traitorous mouth said, "I am indeed flattered by your kind attention. But now, please be so patient as to let me introduce a true convert." I turned and beckoned to Qumax. The worm rumpled out of the jetcopter, his antennae and tentacles wriggling.

"Oh—what is it?" the Rev. Abigail asked.

"A Christian," Qumax said.

"A—a Christian?" Even the rationalization was

beginning to creak under the strain. Qumax was anything but Christian!

"The finest," the worm said, controlling a hiss.

"Really!" The Rev. Abigail was obviously shocked. "A C-Christian, you say?"

"A most enthusiastic convert!" I said. "In fact it may be that he, not I, will lead this world to redemption." I was no Church of the Wood partisan, but I felt a little sick. I began almost to fear that the police were not coming.

"Redemption—Earth?" asked the thoroughly confused preacher.

"Of course," I said. "What better? Who better knows the pitfalls and glories of our world than one who has seen similar? But we're forgetting my assistant. Nancy, if you please, come out here."

"Do you really mean that," she said pitifully.

"I do," I said.

She came, keeping her hands in her pockets.

Three pairs of elderly eyes and a number of younger eyes stared at the coveralls. For a long, long time. Finally Abigail spoke: "Would you— would you care to have something to eat?"

"Certainly," I said, privately appreciating her attempt to change the subject. At least she wasn't jumping on Nancy. Now if only Qumax let well enough alone . . .

"Oh, don't mind those coveralls," I said loftily. *Oh no!* "Those are just the start of Earth's redemption."

"Re-redemption?" Abigail looked as though a very large bone had stuck in her throat.

"That's what it will prove to be," I said. "Evil is in the mind and it must be attacked in the mind—as our wisest ancestors realized. 'Wherefore, if God so clothe the grass of the field, which today is, and tomorrow is cast into the oven, *shall he* not much more *clothe* you, O ye of little faith?' Matthew, chapter six, verse thirty."

"I'm not sure I follow that," she said.

"You will, Reverend Swartz," I said.

"Perhaps," the woman preacher said uneasily, "you would prefer for us to bring you something from the picnic tables. Perhaps some chicken and lemonade?"

"That would be very fine," I said. "But for Brother Qumax, a little something different."

"Oh, yes, of course. What will you have?" she said with commendable grace, turning to Qumax.

"I'll have," Qumax said carefully, "that exotic dish you Earthians call potato chips."

"Potato chips!" exclaimed a young girl's voice, and looking down I beheld a regular Becky Thatcher. She looked back saucily, her freckled nose wrinkling. She stuck out a tongue, licked her lips and remarked with great wisdom, "I *like* potato chips."

"Doesn't everyone?" Qumax said. "Potato chips and—honey, I believe, if you have some?"

"No honey," the little girl said, "but there's soda pop and ice cream."

"Ice cream will do fine," Qumax said, "though I prefer a little sugar on it."

"Sugar on ice cream—that's funny!" said the girl.

"To you, Little Maid," Qumax said. "To me, some of the things humans eat are . . . interesting."

"You're very strange."

"Very."

"Well, we'll bring you your lunch," the Reverend Abigail said awkwardly.

"Fine," Qumax said, "and afterwards we'll speak about redemption."

I lost hope that the police would come. Either this picnic group had been too amazed to tattle, or

Qumax had kept a tight security check while seeming to banter foolishly with children.

"And about my assistant's dress, among other things," I said for Qumax. "After you hear, perhaps you will feel the urge to help spread the word."

Abigail threw one confused, embarrassed glance at Nancy, then turned and walked away, followed by her sister crones. She could choke down a talking alien worm, a pseudo minister, and sacrilege—but an unbagged woman was beyond her tolerance.

Forgotten, the little girl stood gazing up at Qumax. She cleared her throat with what she must have thought was adult solemnity.

"Do you give rides?" the child asked.

"Rides?" For once the big worm was taken aback.

"On your back? Do you charge people to carry them?"

Qumax made his frying sound. He crawled forward. "For you, Little Maid, no charge." His tentacles flicked out, wrapped around the startled girl and lifted her high over his head. His front end came down to ramp level, and there was Becky Thatcher high on a huge green cabbage worm.

"Oh my!" the pretty child said. "Just like a whole handful of elephants!" She meant, of course, the squirming tentacles.

"Better than elephants," Qumax said. "Better than trunks or hands or anything. And those ridges on my belly, they're better than any old legs and are a lot surer footed. Better than anything except—"

"Except what!" she asked happily.

"Wings," he replied, momentarily solemn. "You've got a good hold?"

"Y-yes."

"Then away we go!" And Qumax rumpled off with the most exaggerated up-and-down motion.

It was a measuring worm's crawl, partly, and it was fast, and I knew it was impossible. He was showing off, like the brat he was. Suddenly he slammed on the brakes and began his sidewise sidewinder undulation, also fast and completely incompatible with the inchworm locomotion. Becky was raised up and down, stood still for a moment and then shot forward. She shrieked in joy, clearly not bothered by the incredible contortions.

"Harold?"

"Yes, Nancy?" At least the subject had shifted from her bumps—er, her attire.

"Don't you think we'd better follow them? For the—safety?"

I was surprised again. I would have expected her interest to be on the ride's mechanics. Instead she was acting as though she were Becky's mother.

"Harold?"

I turned my head as the gang of boys raced by. "In your coveralls?" I asked. Then bit my tongue.

"God bless," she swore shockingly, "my bulgy old coveralls! Come on!"

Amen, I added fervently, but mentally.

Without further ado we joined the big parade at the tail. The kids seemed to be having the time of their lives. "Hi-Hi up there!" one of the boys shouted to the girl. "Hang on tight—don't you let go,"

"I won't—for anything!" the little girl said. And then we were winding three times as fast between some trees and there was a purling stream and a song bird's choked off voice and a number of very ordinary people looking up with startled expressions from picnic tables. There was a general cessation of conversation.

Into the breach stepped one Harold Prodkins, now being manipulated as Dr. Andra Moxie, fictitious evangelist extraordinary.

"Behold, Friends," I said, spreading my puppet arms wide and holding my palms high and outwards. "Child of Man and child of Jamborang playing together in peace and friendship. It's a beautiful sight, isn't it?"

There were audibly indrawn breaths. I could imagine what they were thinking: who was I, who was this green thing, and above all who was this delightfully bumpy Jezebel tempting all the men to wicked thoughts just by her appearance? What kind of a Sunday School picnic was this? And then the Head Crone was up and explaining. This was a well-known missionary and his assistant and his convert.

I made a preaching act. I stood up on a picnic table, stepped over the potato salad and cleared my throat. "Friends," I said, "it is high time that we recognize that ours is not a completely hostile universe. There are entire worlds filled with beings such as Qumax—beings who can teach us the supposedly human virtues that are the basis of all Christianity. Friends, do you know what I am talking about? Do you realize that the alien creature you see before you is more pure of heart than most adult Christians? This purity must be accepted, admired, emulated. Only in so far as we succeed in this will we approach the ethical ideal that is the basis of all true Christianity."

I looked out over the heads of my audience. The reverent stillness made me suspect that the worm was exerting himself again—except that he could hardly have much left over after controlling me. Maybe that silence was utter shock. "And how do we attain such purity? Certainly not by concealment. No, concealment and condemnation never have worked and never will work! What we need is the sort of courage displayed here by my assistant. We need to get our minds out of the gutter and cultivate purity of thought, and to do that we need to discard, among other things, that most useless of all affectations—the bag-dress.''

This was worm-talk, not my own—but I found myself agreeing with it. I had often imagined saying something like this to stodgy cousin Freddy ... but had never come close to working up the courage to open my mouth. Qumax wasn't *all* brat ...

I raised my hands commandingly. "Ah yes, I know how you fear to abandon what the excesses of our ancestors seemed to Christian minds to make necessary. But a change of clothing did not make for a change of style, as those who compare present with the past will recognize. Today's attitudes remain much the same as they have always been. It is the attitudes we must change—the attitudes that make for hypocrisy. Too much concealment fosters the very thoughts it is intended to prevent. Yet a sudden drastic change of costume would leave those attitudes untouched. What we must do is work to change the attitude while working slowly at changing the costume. To begin with, there is no reason why ladies may not choose either to wear or not to wear gloves, and why they should not begin to wear something a trifle less all-concealing than the bag-dress. Friends, let us all work to this purpose!"

I put my hands down and beamed benignly at my congregation—and realized sickeningly that the itch was gone from my head, and had been gone for at least a paragraph. *I was doing it myself!* Stage fright smashed me back and I almost fell off the table. I had to get out of here!

I started to step down—and found my left foot in the potato salad. "Friends," I essayed miserably as I scraped off my heel, "let me now conclude only by saying that my two companions and I hope to—to share your repast. We—"

I was interrupted by swelling laughter. The salad had finally toppled onto the ground, and my foot was now nudging a pitcher of cream. I was sharing the repast, all right—with the ants!

Then, blessedly, the itch returned. "Friends," my worm-mouth said, "let me now conclude by saying—" That repetition gave them time to calm down. "That after this delightful interlude we plan to leave immediately for a destination that may surprise you. Dear Friends—" I then paused dramatically while Qumax waited for the suspense to build. "We are on our way to a city that some of you may have cursed as the very stronghold of lewdness. The city, a virtual Sodom if not Gomorrah, holds the Tower of Babel itself. We are going, friends, to Trebvee City, Hooeywood."

Oh no! I thought despairingly. By sheer lucky luck we had somehow avoided detection by Freddy's forces. But now the worm intended to advertise our whereabouts by going on trebvee!

～～～ Chapter 5 ～～～

MUCH talk and food later, we were on our way. Again Warden Nitti piloted, having been revived for this purpose. We provided him with some left-over, foot-squished potato salad for his repast. I almost felt sorry for him, until I remembered how he had treated us at Lucifernia.

As we rose in the air I saw the upturned faces of the three crones, any one of whom might, hours earlier, have carried a flaming faggot to the Jezebel.

Now Nancy made pleasant company during five hours of steady, eventless flying. She basked while I dreamed and Nitti guided the copter silently, and then Big Green Mouth cracked to tell us we were landing.

Nitti parked us gently in a copter-slot before being gassed again, and we waited like company big shots for the men in company uniform. They came, hurrying between copters. They bowed respectfully and opened our doors. "Minister Prodkins, Dr. Dilsmore, Qumax, your studio is waiting for you."

I thought about what it meant as we crossed the lot. Qumax, grossly overconfident after the park scene, must have been busy sending mental signals ahead, forcing government men to pull strings for us and shut up afterwards. It was the only way to travel, I thought. We were doomed, naturally, but the respite had been pleasant.

We entered a large studio. On a sound stage surrounded by cameras and cameramen were grouped table, chairs and a couch. Qumax winked an eye at us and rumpled up to the stage. In back of the cameras sat a small audience seemingly composed entirely of studio executives and government men.

"Minister Prodkins, Dr. Dilsmore—" A man who certainly looked like an executive showed us to some seats in the audience. He flashed an even smile as he sat down. "Exactly on schedule. Just three minutes before the *Face the World* trebcast."

"What do you mean—" I started, but I was afraid I knew. Qumax wouldn't be content to *visit* a trebcast, or to arrange a modest appearance—oh no, he'd have to be right in the middle of the show! My worst fears were being realized.

Alvin Swept walked on stage right then. Following close on his heels were three men in conservative suits. All took chairs. Two other men joined the group, then a sixth; the last wore a broad white collar with no opening in front. Following the priest came a Jewish rabbi, an African, three Orientals and an Arab. All took seats.

A light flashed. Cameras dollied onto invisible chalk marks. A large sign lit with the words ON THE AIR.

"Ladies and Gentlemen," said the barely seated Alvin, "the World Broadcasting Network in cooperation with the Planetary News Service takes pleasure in presenting LIVE this highly special edition of *Face the World*! There will be no interruptions for commercials and no set time limit on what promises to be the interview of the century. Paying for this—one might almost say extemporaneous—trebcast is the world government itself. This is of course unprecedented, even in time of elections.

"But, ladies and gentlemen, this trebcast is unprecedented in another way. When in the entire history of the human species have representatives of all the world's major religions gotten together to instruct a visitor from another planet on the subject of Earth's religions? It's astonishing—I would never have believed that we would see such a thing in this generation. Ladies and gentlemen, I'm a little overwhelmed. I haven't been allowed to prepare myself ahead of time with so much as an organized outline. Approximately ten minutes ago I was informed suddenly by a call directly from the chairman of the World Communications Commission and another surprise call from a quote high official in world government unquote that this historical trebcast would be made. Perhaps now the best thing I can do is simply turn the opening explanation over to the being who is making this all possible. Ladies and gentlemen, Brother Qumax, visitor to Earth from Jamborango, a world near the cultural center of our galaxy!"

There was, I was sure, consternation inside and outside the studio—wherever human beings saw the trebcast. And Freddy would be literally gnashing his teeth. This was going to be awful!

The cameras dollied in. Qumax vibrated antennae, looked with shoe-button eyes into the lens, and spoke:

"For the purpose of comparing the tenets of Earth religions with other and older faiths . . ."

I could see what he was trying to do, but the worm had really overreached himself this time. He expected to read these men's innermost thoughts, feelings and desires and make all hostility vanish. He thought he could publicly examine and re-examine every major premise of religion and turn it inside out with unprecedented respect for logic. He thought there would be a weeping, head-shaking gravely stricken panel led by one grotesquely smiling Qumax. A trebethon to end trebethons—the whole world and all trebvee-receiving planets would be gasping and wondering and trying to digest the sweat-drenched hours of theological agonizing. A really historic occurrence—of that he had no doubt.

For a while I almost thought he could pull it off. He argued, by impressive examples picked from the minds of the clerics, that all the differences did not amount to the mountains man had made of them. Molehills, not mountains—and sometimes not even molehills. Among the star civilizations, he said, there were many religions and many proponents of every conceivable viewpoint. There were faiths that could be classified as prolife and others as antilife, prointellect and antiintellect. Qumax claimed to be representing nothing—only drawing examples for clarifying parallels.

Oh yes, he tried. He pointed out that all ethical teachings were based on one premise: that it is better to live in such a way as to be free from the torments of unethical conduct. With that to go on, there should be united cooperation and a blurring of dissimilarities. Why wasn't there? Why should all ethical strivings on the planet Earth lead to internecine warfare? Wasn't the species of man sane enough to *see* that molehills didn't matter when there were mountains to climb? Why didn't the individuals quit pretending that so much mattered that didn't matter? Why didn't the human species learn responsibility, as the creatures of the galaxy had?

I was enthralled in spite of myself, but Nancy shook her head negatively. I watched the clerics and felt sorry for them and thrilled for them, sure that for the first time in centuries such as these were learning answers with the strength of revelations. But Nancy was watching Qumax sadly. I thought that man might change now—practice and preaching, the old eternal conflict. Change and variety were among the most unchanging facts of the universe. Dogmatism simply wasn't justified from any ethically based standpoint. Accept it, human species, and get on with the business of facing the universe. But Nancy frowned.

Only gradually did I perceive certain truths, and perhaps I never grasped the whole of it. Perhaps it was that these men were by no means innocent picnickers, but trained, experienced debaters who knew how to deal with sacrilege by their definitions. Perhaps it was that they instinctively unified in the face of this challenge to all their parameters. Perhaps it was that they did not *want* to change their lifelong beliefs—beliefs on which they made their respective livings. But mainly I think it was that *religion is not based on logic.* Qumax was trying to use logic to make points that were more in the realm of emotion, spirit and faith. And so he failed.

Qumax was a child. He simply could not appreciate the depth of commitment these men had. He succeeded only in baffling himself. Thus, abruptly, the program came to a close. With bad grace the worm terminated it before his naiveté became apparent to all.

"But be of good cheer, Friends," Qumax said

with feigned equanimity. "For tonight there's a big treat in store. Tonight, ladies and gentlemen—" He paused dramatically, recovering some of his normal zest for mischief. "Tonight there's a program none of you will want to miss—"

I looked at Nancy. Nancy looked at me. What could it be? We'd all be unbearably lucky if we stayed clear of Lucifernia that long, for now the whole world knew where Qumax was. What possible revelation could be worth such colossal risk?

"Tonight I, Qumax, will present a dramatic farspace adventure that I will both direct and star in. Included in the cast will be none other than your real-life Minister of Inner-Galactic World Affairs, Minister Harold W. Prodkins. . . ."

Ouch! The worm was taking it out on *me!* The bad-sport juvenile brat!

"Tune in tonight, Friends, for a thrilling Captain Cloud adventure!"

Captain Cloud—trebvee idol of the adolescent masses. My adult brain knew he was merely the stage name of a nonentitious actor, Stanley Stanslovitch; but my boyhood memory proclaimed him as *the* hero of all time. What were we in for now?

As though the announcement itself were not sufficiently inane and shocking, a localized commotion arose within the studio audiences. "Goodness!" and then "Golly Gee!" in teenage timbre. Impelled by these unnatural sounds, I turned quickly and discovered the tall robust figure of Stanley Stanslovitch, Captain Cloud himself.

"Mr. Stanslovitch!" I exclaimed before catching myself. I stared at his twin blaster-guns and wondered where his famed Texas drawl might be.

"Hi ya, Space Partners," he said. And yes, there it was, all sagebrush and steershit. It was illogical but I felt as excited as a six-year-old.

But of course I was a grown, mature, adult man now. Hardly a gushing fan. It behooved me to address him with appropriate dignity. "Mr. Stanslovitch," I said, and took another breath. "I'm sure you know who we are and I'm sure you're not thrilled, but believe me *I'm* thrilled ever since I was a little kid well for years anyhow—"

He glanced benignly at me as my balloon exhausted its air. "It's the hairdye," he remarked. "That and the wrinkle-cream."

"Oh, I didn't mean to imply—I mean only—uh—"

"It doesn't matter. You all want my autograph?" He already had produced a gold celebrity pen.

"Certainly," I said. I searched my empty pockets, then held out a sleeve of my borrowed shirt. "Just sign here," I mumbled awkwardly.

"Shore." Evidently he was used to this sort of thing. One moment the pen was posed and the next it was making pretty pink, gold and silver lines. As soon as he finished, I took my sleeve and looked at it. The autograph read: "Stanley Stanslovitch, the one and only C-A-P-T-A-I-N C-L-U-D."

"Uh, Mr. Stanslovitch—uh, shouldn't there be an 'O' in that?"

"Why, shore." With gray eyes twinkling he converted the letters and hyphens of the last two words to a colorful line and printed other letters above. "And don't," he warned, "ask me to change it again. Enough is enough, Partner."

"Oh, I won't, Mr. Stanslovitch," I said. Then I looked at the change. The autograph now read: ". . . the one and only C-A-P-T-A-I-N C-L-O-D."

Qumax humped to the edge of the rostrum. "I'm going to need some personnel," he announced. "In addition to stagehands, electricians and stenographers, I'm going to need some of you actors. Stanley Stanslovitch, get Priscilla Prentiss, your leading lady, and meet me in Studio Five."

"Yes sir, Mr. Qumax!" said Stanslovitch. For all his being an actor, he responded rather well. I was wondering just what Qumax had planned for the rest of us, and not at all certain we would like it when we found out.

Suddenly there was a studio page at my elbow. "Mr. Prodkins—you're wanted on the v-phone." Then, swallowing a suddenly bobbing Adam's apple, the young hopeful actor added, "It's the President, sir. President of the World! His personal secretary spoke for him!"

"Pruneface. Well that's great," I said.

"Pardon, sir?"

"Thanks for the message." I wondered if I should say what I really felt about the honor. Last time my cousin had phoned it had been a trap.

"You can take the call in private, sir."

"Thank you," I said. "That will of course be best." I stood up and offered Nancy my arm, hoping she would take it and lend me the needed moral support.

"I'm with you every step of the way, Space Partner," she whispered. Her arm hooked into mine with a familiarity I had hardly anticipated—almost a proprietary gesture. We walked behind the page, entered a private office together and found ourselves facing a v-phone. The page left, closing the door behind him.

I moved to the v-phone and my presence activated the screen, bringing on the image of Pruneface first, and then the President. I studied Freddy Bascum's face with care, marveling that he was just an ordinary man after all who was maybe scared to death at this moment. I wondered what the interview would bring.

"Mr. Minister, I must admit that I was favorably impressed by the trebcast."

"You . . . liked it . . . Mr. President?"

"It was adroit. Until the end."

His way of saying that Qumax had made an utter fool of himself. I pretended not to comprehend. "You didn't like the announcement?"

"I think the announcement may call for rather drastic care, H—Mr. Minister. I'm wondering whether I can, after all, count on you to ease the brakes on?"

I wondered why he felt constrained to beg this way. Why didn't he just send in the troops? Then I realized that we had preempted the stage from the doubles he had planted, and that now it would be exceedingly awkward to remove us without giving his prior machinations away. Who would double for Qumax, now? Probably the worm had counted on this to prevent any overt measures against us. Personally, I wouldn't have trusted Freddy that far.

So now the President of the World was ready to play along with us, provided we calmed down the display. Maybe we'd get out of this mess with intact integuments after all. "Um, I see what you mean. You think that I should control Qumax."

"Precisely. For the good of Earth and your own possible future political career."

"Frankly, Mr. President," I said loftily, "I haven't been thinking about politics."

Freddy frowned. "Everything will be made right," he said. "Just so you do your job now and forget about that little unpleasantness. Count it—simply a misunderstanding between relatives?"

He was pushing it too far. "You'd better watch your step, *Mr.* President. I don't take kindly to—"

"Mr. President," Nancy said hurriedly, "there's

something—excuse me, both of you, but I just wanted to remind you. Qumax hasn't entered my mind yet. I think if anyone can control him or interfere with him if necessary, that I—"

"You'd, eh, dispose of him, Dr. Dilsmore?"

"Goodness no, Mr. President!" Nancy sounded shocked.

"The Swarm Tyrant would really love that," I muttered. "Then he'd have real cause to play Solar Pool with the real solar system . . ."

"Precisely," Freddy agreed. "We must be diplomatic."

"I think I can interfere if necessary," Nancy said, "and tell the public what Qumax is really about."

"Really about, Dr. Dilsmore?"

"A let's pretend game."

"Oh—yes, Dr. Dilsmore. And then the innergalactic ship will be here soon and we can straighten out anything that requires government straightening. Yes, I do believe that might work."

"You look," I observed, "as though you are calling off an execution."

The President blanched. So some such temptation *had* trotted through his brain. Qumax was in no danger, of course, for the threat of his Swarm Tyrant could not be ignored. But those of us whom the worm was using as props . . . maybe. Nancy's freak ability to defy the alien just might be the saving of us.

"Mr. Minister," said the President decisively, "I am putting you and Dr. Dilsmore in full charge. I want you to know that I—that I'll be available any time of the day or night if you need help. The entire resources of the world government stand at your immediate disposal."

"I—" Mentally I cursed him. "I won't forget your kind cooperation, Mr. President."

Thought furrowed the politician's forehead. *Hidden meaning? Hidden meaning?* I might have heard. Lucky I couldn't read his complex, ruthless mind; I'd probably be sickened. "All right, Mr. Minister and Dr. Dilsmore," he said finally. "To each of us our jobs. That's understood and accepted, isn't it?"

"It is, Mr. President," I said.

"Fine. Goodbye, Mr. Minister, Dr. Dilsmore."

"Goodbye, Mr. President," Nancy and I said. The screen blanked.

I marched to the large desk in the office and plumped down, weak with something like relief. I opened the drawer, searching for some tissues to wipe my face. I found—a bottle. And several clean glasses. Expensive, potent distillation.

"I'll take some of that," Nancy said.

"I didn't know you drank!"

"I don't," she said, holding forth a glass. "But I was bluffing. I don't think I can control Qumax at all. All I can do is resist him—so far."

I popped the cork and poured her one, and followed with a dose of my own. She was right—we weren't out of this morass by a long shot. The worm was planning some horrendous show involving Captain Cloud and who knew what else, and it would surely snap Freddy's suspenders and we'd all be in dire peril. Caught between Qumax and Freddy—and neither, realistically, could be pacified.

"Harold—" she said after a bit. "The responsibility you and I share—it's very great, isn't it?"

"It's the greatest," I said, invoking my gift for understatement. I noticed with surprise that the fluid level was down more than it ought to be, in the bottle. But my problems did not seem nearly so pressing.

"Harold—these coveralls . . .

"Delightful," I said. *Sinful too,* I thought with a certain illicit pleasure.

"Harold, eh, could you"—she threw a glance at the door—"maybe help me get some clothing that's a little more, eh, conventional?"

So her most fundamental concern was not the President or the worm, but her unbagged state. Her dishabille. "If that's what you want," I said.

She looked at me with doubt in her eyes. "After that speech you made?"

"After the speech Qumax made me make."

She frowned, vaguely disappointed perhaps, and sipped at her glass again. "It made sense, that speech. But with all these ugly bumps showing—"

"Not ugly," I said. "I—like coveralls on you. Really, Nancy."

She blushed. I knew that I must be blushing. What had just passed seemed horribly profound.

"Eh, Harold, if you'd rather I didn't . . . ?"

"I want—I mean I *like* the way you are," I said. The bottle seemed to be empty.

"Would you—would you do me a favor? Would you help me, please, decorate these?"

"Decorate? How?"

She looked about and spotted a celebrity pen behind the phone. "Here!" she said, making a couple of swipes before she managed to grasp it. "Those lovely colored lines—could you, please?"

"You mean draw? To make you look like a baggie? I mean, like—" I fumbled about verbally for another moment, then gave up. "I'm sorry but I've never—never drawn."

"Well—design, then." The bulges in her coverall tops rose and fell. She righted the pen, laid her coveralled arm on the desk and poised the pen over her forearm. Quickly she drew a sloppy crosshatch.

I stared. "Tick-tack-toe?"

She made an *O* in an upper left square and handed the pen to me. "I called it cat-and-mouse," she said.

I made an *X*. "It's a very pretty color," I said.

She *O*-ed.

I *X*-ed.

She *O*-ed and crossed a line through it.

We began a new game.

She *X*-ed.

I *O*-ed.

She *X*-ed.

I *O*-ed.

She *X*-ed.

I *O*-ed and crossed a line through it.

The games became more interesting as they marched up her sleeve and around her shoulder. Much more interesting. With a change of board, there was more and more care required, longer periods of deliberation. But somehow my concentration suffered. That is, I concentrated very hard, but kept losing the games. Soon, approaching a top bulge, I dropped the pen and tried kissing her. To my astonishment she responded immediately.

"Oh, Harold," she sighed. "Harold, my—my darling!"

I found my arms around her. I tightened them and I thought that as she breathed her bulges were flattening. Her blue eyes looked at me in a tender way and I knew that it was going to hurt her to slap me. For she was going to have to slap me. Her entire upbringing would demand it. And the strange part of it was that I wanted her to—for that was part of a decent upbringing. It was a real necessity that she slap me, I felt.

"All right, you Earthian loafers," my mouth said. "It's time you come to the studio for rehearsal. My play, *The Alien Viewpoint*, is undoubtedly a masterpiece."

I was suddenly sober again—and horrified.

"Damn you!" Nancy said, looking pretty sober herself. And then, to my indescribable joy, she really walloped me.

Chapter 6

WE left the unnatural privacy of the office and found our way through halls bustling with actors and actresses—many of whom eyed or commented on the scientist's lack of a proper bag-dress—to Studio Five. Qumax and staff were waiting there for us. I glanced at a clock as we came in and learned with surprise that we had enjoyed privacy for almost three hours. Then I did another take, because the time was *wrong*. We had left the picnic of the Church of the Wood, way back east, around two in the afternoon. The copter journey here had taken five hours, and the Trebvee religious panel a couple more. Our three hours tick, tack, toeing Nancy's coveralls (and oh, yes—there had been Freddy's call in there somewhere too!) should bring us up to midnight. But it was only nine—prime viewing time.

Then I remembered: we had traveled three time zones west. That accounted for the loss. We had *spent* those hours, but they wouldn't register on the local clocks. Stupid me!

"There won't be time for rehearsals," Qumax said, not quite enigmatically. "Since I will be aiding each of you to act your finest, there is no necessity that you do anything so crude as to memorize lines. To save time, I'll just explain what each of you will be doing and why."

He explained, briefly and to the point: where we would enter and exit, how we would work our vocal cords, what special effects there would be. It sounded like a Captain Cloud adventure written with somewhat alien tongue in cheek.

"I don't know, Qumax," I said. "This sounds as though you're trying to make a point, but the point is, I fear, alien. Remember that religious—"

"*You* remember it; I have a weak alien stomach," he said cheerfully. "No matter about the rest. You'll learn as we go along. Places, everyone!"

I found myself pushed back behind some scenery in the company of a strange starlet. No, not so strange, I realized. Priscilla Prentice! That girl wore a baggie as no one ever had worn a baggie! In short, she wore it over a phony spacesuit.

"Passion Jenny," I said, admiring mentally the well-hidden curves I had so often tried to visualize. "Could you—would you—will you please?"

She looked shocked. "Not *here*, lover. We need privacy."

I wasn't certain what she had in mind, but I felt the flush push up my neck and blotch my face. I thrust out my sleeve and indicated the Captain Cloud autograph and handed her the celebrity pen I had brought with me from the office.

"Oh," she said, disappointed. Then she recovered herself and smiled dazzlingly. "Why of course, Mr. Probkins."

She took the pen, lowered her eyes in a way calculated to make a man's stomach squeeze against his liver. "I'm honored to be autographing someone so"—sex-smile—"important."

I watched her write "Priscilla Prentice, the one and only PASSION JENNY," and felt my heart kick out. I wondered just why she was finding it necessary to move so close while she signed, why her fingers pressed harder than need be and trembled with the slightest hint of indecency, why she could have use for such nearly intoxicating perfume inside that inner spacesuit.

"There you are," she whispered huskily in a way that I felt certain was contrived, but that still palpitated my coronary organ. "That *was* all you wanted—*wasn't* it?"

"Miss Prentice—" I said.

"Dressing room twelve," she whispered. "I'll be alone there after the trebcast. Surely you can spare me just a *little* time?"

I swallowed, the all-world boy beset by a temptation he had never anticipated. "I—I—"

Her fingers squeezed my arm with astonishing intimacy. "I'll look for you," she whispered.

If she could be that sexy in a spacesuit topped by a baggie, I thought, my mouth salivating guiltily, what would she be like in the *nude?* Did I dare find out?

Lights flashed. People moved and cameras turned. I found myself waiting in place with nothing more interesting to gaze upon than a trebvee monitor. I watched the play, trying not to make comparisons between the actress and the extraterrestrialogist.

On the screen: Announcement of Captain Cloud adventure—unsponsored and uninterrupted. Play: *The Alien Viewpoint.* Play's author: Qumax of Jamborango. Play's director: Qumax of Jam. Play's star: Q of J. Filmed clip of exterior of Captain Cloud's ship, *The Texas Rose.* Cut to ship's interior—

an on-stage mockup. Present: a slightly glazed-of-eye Captain Cloud and his beloved space-flower pure-as-the-Texas-snow—Passion Jenny. Jenny of course had on gloves. She was pulling at them in what might have been uncontrollable nervousness.

"Captain Cloud," Jenny said, "we are now further into the galaxy than any humans have ever penetrated. All thanks to the inner-galactic drive you've had installed."

"Yes," Cloud said. "How clever it was of me to take advantage of that unsophisticated alien."

"And we'll be seeing it soon, won't we, Captain—the real civilization that exists near the heart of our galaxy?"

"I expect," said the Captain. "How's the Minister of Earth's Inner-Galactic World Affairs doing?"

"Still asleep," she said, "like most Earth officials. He was really surprised when you yanked him away from his pool table and brought him out here."

"Yes," Cloud said contentedly. "It's supposed to be his job to deal with inner-galactics on behalf of Earth. But we know, you and I, that it's only the adventurers who have a chance to deal with far strangers. When did a politician ever get out and make the initial contacts?"

"When indeed," said Passion. "But then our Minister isn't really in politics. That was why the constitutional amendment was passed—to keep the responsibility out of politics."

"Hogwash!" said Cloud. "Politics and politicians—ugh, I'm just glad I've got the old *Flower*."

"I'm glad too," she said. "Cloud?"

"Huh, Passion?"

"It's so hot in here and we're so far from Earth—don't you think I might shuck these gloves?"

"Shuck away," Cloud said.

Passion peeled first the right and then the left glove. She discarded these modesties in a seat. Her hands—naked now as the Texas dawn—were pale drab creatures that had never known sunlight. I was embarrassed for her exposure.

"Cloud?"

"Yes, Passion,"

"We're so far from Earth and its brutal, disgusting ways—don't you think that I might shed this hot, uncomfortable bag-dress?"

"Shed away, my Little Flower."

Passion raised her arms and pulled off the baggie. Underneath was the spacesuit that should have been cut a lot like Nancy's coveralls. Only unseen modifications had been made: instead of sleeves and legs the garment simply had holes from which the arms and legs emerged. Passion's arms were skinny, her legs more so. I knew that this was a daring thing, but I felt vaguely disappointed by it. Nancy's limbs, in contrast, had been quite—

"Captain Cloud?"

"Yes, Passion." Cloud eyed his little flower with only slight interest as she folded the dress in the middle and hung it over the seat back. This was, his expression implied, only routine for this kind of flight.

"We're so far from Earth and its irrational, prohibiting ways, don't you think that—"

"No, Passion," Cloud said. "As long as there are people who could be shocked by your dear, bare skin, I think it better that you leave on the costume."

"People?"

"The Minister is from Earth, Passion my Texas Flower. Though you may be pure as purest air, there is something about Earth-minds that will make you feel impure. You wouldn't really want the Minister to admit that he's not a bold and realistic adventurer?"

"I"—pouty face—"guess not, Captain."

"Things will be better soon for both of us. Soon Earth will discard the silly affectation of the bagdress. When it does, maybe there will be an end to a lot of pretense."

"I hope so, Captain. It's so difficult pretending you haven't a body. No one *wants* to think of bodies all the time, but with so much reminding us . . ." She trailed off as I walked in, ostensibly from the other compartment.

"My, I've had a *good* sleep!" I said for Qumax. "And you are looking well, Passion—very well." Privately I thought her pipe-stem extremities would better have remained concealed under the baggie. In her case, the suggestion was considerably more potent than the reality.

"And you must look," she said, "because your conditioning is such that you cannot help yourself. You must look and say to yourself not 'Here is a woman' but 'Here is a—'"

"Look there!" Cloud interrupted her. "There on the screen—other ships!"

"My goodness, it looks like a battle!" Passion said.

"A war?" I said, as though the Minister of Earth's Inner-Galactic World Affairs should naturally be the last to know. "These superior beings?"

"Everything is superior to something," Cloud said wisely. "Look, one ship is chasing the others! I do believe—yes, it's coming back and—now it's pacing us. We're going to have boarders—invaders!"

"Maybe not invaders," I said. From offstage came suitable sound effects: the presumed noises of a spaceship grappling in a hard vacuum. There were clangs and bangs and thumps, anyway.

"Oh, it wants in!" Passion said, fluttering her naked hands.

"I'll open the airlock," I said.

"No!" Cloud commanded. "That is—wait until I get my blasters out."

"You leave those blasters where they are!" I said. "You hero types always shoot first and question later. We responsible cowards can't afford to risk misunderstanding." I jerked a lever on the dummy panel. Whines and clangs sounded and slowly a fake airlock opened up. There stood Qumax, complete with ridiculous wrinkle-covering space-suit. He flicked a tentacle to a control located just beneath his helmet. There was a burst of sound from his artificial speaker-box.

"Greetings, Earth-things! I have just saved your tight skins from a fleet of Strumbermian pirates. For this you were about to reward me in a fashion typically Earthian. But thanks to the Minister of Earth's Inner-Galactic World Affairs, Captain Cloud does not get to fire off his blasters."

"You mean—?" Cloud said.

"Yes," Qumax said. "Peace and prosperity forever—assuming Earthians can keep from killing each other and from joining with Strumbermian pirates in their ceaseless depredations. That, however, is assuming a lot—knowing how addicted humans are to slaughter. Yes, indeed, Earth friends . . ."

A sudden onslaught of noise offstage cut off what Qumax was saying.

"Jupegas—Jupegas—invasion!" someone screamed. The cry was Nancy's. She came pounding on stage as though out to set a track record, completely oblivious of the set and the cameras and the fact that Qumax had not written a part for her.

"Harold—Harold!" she shouted, spying me. "You've got to do something! Qumax—those troops!"

Passion's unscripted scream all but burst my ear drums. She was looking past the bright trebvee lights, eyes and mouth wide.

"The camera crew—the camera crew!" Passion screeched. "The camera crew's asleep!" She leaped to her feet and ran offstage, screaming. Apparently that was the one horror with which she could not begin to cope: a nonfunctioning camera crew.

"That's what I'm trying to tell you," Nancy said. "Qumax, you must—" and then she lapsed into colorlessness and tumbled senseless.

I left the dumbfounded Stanley Stanslovitch and ran to her side. Just as I reached her, Qumax took hold of me and made me turn to see the broad wink he was making. Beside him I saw the sprawled-out actor who had played Cloud, and I saw that Qumax's green face was now covered by a transparent helmet. And something else I saw—something that scared the shock out of me. Several tall and mean-looking men were advancing on Qumax with drawn gas-guns.

Then the significance of the gas-masks on the men's faces hit me just as I realized that there was a smoking gas-grenade lying at Nancy's elbow. That couldn't be Jupegas!

I reached for the grenade. My fingers touched it. All went black.

"Harold," Nancy whispered urgently. "I—I think we're being followed."

Huh? Hadn't I been through this before?

"Not quite," Qumax said. "I have just rescued you and given you failing humans the antidote. But it was a bit sticky getting away clean; those government men are tough. So now I need you to keep watch for the pursuit while I apply evasive maneuvers."

I looked dazedly about me. Nitti was at the controls again, and Nancy and Qumax and I were riding in the copter. It was as though the Hooey-wood experience had never happened—except that Nancy wore coveralls decorated with tick-tack-toe crosshatches.

"Harold," she said, "I—I think they're shooting!"

Naturally! I thought. Straining my head around, I could see the bright flashes emerging from the approaching copter. They *were* shooting!

"Freddy!" I cried. "The double-crossing bastard! He said he'd let us do it our own way." But of course I had been a fool to think I could trust my cousin in political matters. He had merely allayed our fears while preparing a decisive counterstrike. But the worm had been alert, and had done his usual stunts to get us all back to the copter. Probably he had taken over the mind of the leader of the commando party. . . .

The copter zig-zagged, throwing us about. I hoped one of those bright flashes did not take our rotors off. Qumax had miscalculated again, and could hardly stop a shot that had already been fired.

But they didn't have the range yet. "Douse the lights!" I cried. "We might lose them in the dark—"

And what would *we* crash into, blind? I didn't know our elevation, but it couldn't be much.

"Oh, more ships!" said Nancy.

I saw their light now—behind us, to either side, and in front. We were englobed!

"Phone Freddy!" I said. "Tell him that if they shoot us down, it'll kill the worm too!" But I had little hope. Obviously some hotheads were in charge locally, and they would have us in ashes before reasonable controls were instituted.

Then the lights began to waver and fade. Clouds!

But not the usual kind. These glowed, lighting the entire area around us. The thicker they became, the more light there was. I had never seen an effect like this, and I didn't much appreciate it now.

"Almost there," Qumax said. The copter began to climb. The surrounding mist took on an ugly greenish hue rather like the worm's tail, and I didn't like it. This was too much like swimming, and I feared reefs.

"Almost where?" Nancy inquired.

"Good Lord!" That was me, I think.

For a great green bulb-shape had appeared directly in front of us. It looked to be as high as a fifty story building and as big around as a forty-apartment-per-floor condominium. I suppose it was reflection from its surface that gave the adjacent cloud its color. Indeed, the entire opacity might stem from the vapors I now observed spouting from vents in this object's lower surface.

We were headed right for it at full speed.

"Stop!" Nancy cried, alarmed.

We slowed, but continued to approach. It was exactly as though we were coming in for a landing—except that we were a mile or so above the ground, and the landing field was vertical. The eerily gleaming wall came closer, closer—*what was it?*

In a moment we would crash against it. The rotors would smash, and we would fall—one tiny gnat crushed against the abdomen of this grotesquely swollen firefly! I wanted to shut my eyes, but could not.

A mouth opened: a ponderous metal orifice revealing inner teeth of glowing gold. And we sailed through the portals and cut our rotors. We bumped gently and then we were at peace.

Landed.

Inside the open cargo-lock of an alien and utterly strange space ship!

~~~~~~~~~~ **Chapter 7** ~~~~~~~~~~

So this was it! We were aboard an inner-galactic
cargo ship without the knowledge or consent of
either Earthly or Jamborango-ly authorities. We
had kidnapped, not the worm we claimed, but the
wardens of Earth's most notorious prison. So now
Nancy and I were in real trouble with our world,
and Qumax, playing hooky, would have a fancy
time wiggling out of and accounting to his terrible
Swarm Tyrant.

It would have been better to have left well enough
alone. Had I gone along with Freddy's original
plan. . . .

Yet for all that I discovered I was not sorry. I
had stood on my rights and the rights of Earth, and
I still had a mission to complete. Somehow. Now I
was the first Earthman to stand aboard an Inner-
Galactic Space Ship. Nancy was the first Earth-
woman. And Nitti was the first Earthwarden, un-
deserving as he was. It was worth it!

What was that black spidery thing crawling
towards us?

The creature paused and seemed to be directing the heads of two green snakes at our copter. A vapor was issuing from the snakes' mouths and rising up around us. It was, I realized belatedly, some sort of gas.

"Qumax—what?" I asked, stepping back.

The worm stirred and made a teakettle hiss. A chuckle. "Just a little disinfecting is all. You Earthians are horribly unclean. Germs, viruses, fungus, pollen, grime—I don't know how you stand that contaminated bath you live in. This will cure it, though. And that's a freight-handler—what you'd call a robot."

"Are you sure that stuff is harmless to us?" Nancy asked worriedly. "We *need* some of our viruses to live. Our differing metabolism—"

"I'm *not* sure," Qumax said, and hissed merrily. "Sometimes it turns aliens into mottled jelly. And I suggest you watch your step when you get out— the floors here are coated with gravite."

"Gravite?" I asked stupidly.

"What your scientists—laughable as any such designation may be when applied to the techniques of such primitives—would call a polarity-reversing plastic. It makes for easier crawling."

It seemed to me that a brat showing off his civilization was even more bratlike than one trapped on a primitive planet. But I was the first to step down. Suddenly I found myself tumbling slow-motion across the floor. I landed softly on my fundament a dozen feet from the copter, disheveled but unhurt. Except for my pride.

"I told you to watch the gravite!" Qumax called, and went into another paroxysm of sizzling.

I was too intrigued by the novelty of antigravity to be angry. Here I seemed to weigh only a few pounds. It took some getting used to. For one thing, my stomach felt biliously light. For another, my lifetime conditioning to Earth gravity caused me to put far more muscle into moving than was necessary or wise here, but it was pleasantly easy after a moment.

The others stepped down far more cautiously, though the warden bobbled like a helium balloon for a moment before catching his balance. He looked even fatter in fractional gravity than he had on land, since he could now bulge freely in every direction. He didn't say anything.

We followed a small floating guide-robot through an anteroom and into an oversized airlock. I realized that in deep space the entire intake chamber would be in hard vacuum. As we left it I looked back to see the huge entry port closing.

The guide-robot—no more than a lighted ball with retractable arms—floated to a receptacle and became quiescent beside a row of similar units. We passed on through to the inner iris of the lock and emerged into a brightly colored salon stuffed with alien furniture. Who on Earth would use such paraphernalia? I had never before seen such a mismatched collection.

"You are wondering," said Qumax, "about the accoutrements. Simple—there is more than one race aboard, and most aren't humanoid, fortunately. Jams aren't the only inner-galactic life you'll encounter."

"Is there," Nancy inquired almost timidly, "a captain? Someone in charge?"

"Why not?" Qumax said grandly. He looked past me. "Captain Fuzzpuff, allow me to introduce three local primitives."

I turned to see a three-foot bug balanced on spindly hind legs.

"Captain—?" I said for want of anything better.

At home I stepped on roaches (Freddy had been wrong about my not hurting a fly), and suddenly I feared a roach would step on *me*.

"At your service," the bug said in slight whistling tones. "Captain Fuzzpuff of the *Comet's Tail* at your service."

"Captain," I said, overwhelmed. "How is it you know our language?"

"Doesn't take long," the bug said. "Not when you learn to apply what your species calls telepathy."

Telepathy! Qumax had warned me, but it hadn't sunk in. The bug must have been reading my mind the very moment I was thinking of—

"Do not be concerned," Fuzzpuff said with what must have been a smile. A mandibular smile. "At home we step on humanoids."

I decided to act while the acting was good. "Captain, I need to speak with someone in authority. My world, Earth, has business with Jamborango."

"That would be wise, since you are traveling with a Jam prince. It isn't convenient to place a call at the moment, but once you reach Jamborango you will be able to speak for yourself."

"But I'm not going to—"

"You have little choice, I fear. Your companion Qumax specified that you were to accompany him the entire distance, and we are already underway. My schedule does not permit a reapproach to Earth at this stage."

I looked at Qumax. *You worm*, I thought with mixed alarm, fury and amazement. *What have you gotten us into?*

I thought the frying pan was about to catch fire. As if I hadn't known already how funny such a brat would find such a practical joke.

"Captain," Nancy said quickly, "could we have a

look at your ship? We've never been aboard such a vessel before."

"Certainly," he said graciously. "If you will follow—?"

We followed. I was glad for the respite from the need to make any decision. I could not really believe that we were in deep space, for only a few moments had passed and I had not felt any acceleration. But *if we were*—

We marched down a corridor, made a turn to the right, and almost bumped into two aliens with the facial features of bulldogs. "Passengers," the captain explained. "They happen to be Yabarians. I am Pmpermian. Just as the three of you are Earthian, and Qumax is Jamborangian."

"But not just *any* Jam," Qumax said, sizzling happily.

I looked at Nancy and Nitti, noticing the curious way their nostrils flared. There were bound to be alien smells, I thought, besides Qumax's licorice.

Another corner and other passengers. While this new pair were still some distance away I had the impression of approaching Mae Wests. Not until we closed the gap did I see that their faces were decidedly simian. As we passed I saw smoky eyes in the masks of light reddish facial hair, perceived that the breasts—really, there was no more decent word—were astonishingly conical, and noted long fleshy pinkish tails. The upper structures were covered by garments not unlike coverall-tops, and the lowers by short skirts; but I had the impression of nakedness and indecency.

These two were conversing in low gurgles. But drowning sounds were the least of what bothered me. As I saw those sensual lips shape and peeked at those hairless bare tails protruding from the too-brief skirts, I felt that I was gazing at something shockingly lewd. It distressed me profoundly. I feared that too many seconds of such sights would affect a normal man's posture. Yet these were aliens, having no affinity to human beings.

I did not trust myself to speak. *Qumax—those things—?*

There are many species aboard, as I told you, Rube, Qumax thought disinterestedly. *Some close to yours, others not so close. These are Prunians.*

"This is telepathy!" I exclaimed.

"You'll learn to maintain a mindshield eventually," Qumax said, "so you won't be embarrassed by untoward thought directed at you." *Prunians close enough for you, Earthian?* "Nancy Dilsmore does now; in fact, she can neither receive nor send. Since I had possession of your mind for a time, I opened certain new channels to facilitate communication, though you still need practice. Once you get on to it, you'll find that languages are easily learned," *How about the cute one on the left—real piece of tail there, no?* "since you pick up the meaning, not the alien shape or sound."

One day I would gladly strangle a certain neckless alien brat!

"And of course there are rules of courtesy about such things," Fuzzpuff said. "Privacy of thought is highly valued. Once I mastered your spoken language, I did not intrude in your mind again."

Unlike a certain worm! I fired at Qumax.

"I never felt any itch," I said to Fuzzpuff.

"There is no discomfort in telepathy," the captain said. "Mind *control* is another matter, however. But few galactic species possess that capability, fortunately."

Qumax sizzled.

Fuzzpuff's head turned around—all the way

around—until it was on backwards. "On this deck," he continued comfortably, "we have all the living quarters. Below is the cargo hold, most of the freight handlers, the engine room and the ship's workshops. Cargo accounts for a high percentage of the *Comet's Tail*'s mass, however. You may view the unloading operations upon disembarking. Passengers are prohibited below decks without official clearance. This is for safety—of both cargo and passengers."

"Are there, um, lifeboats?" I asked.

"Certainly. But ours have never been used. The only real danger in deep space for a ship such as this one is the unlikely chance of being set upon by a Strumbermian raider."

"Pirates?" Nancy asked, and Nitti seemed to perk up.

"They very rarely annoy licensed ships, though they have been getting bolder recently. Strumbermians have hitherto preferred attacking craft who fly the colors of worlds not party to the Inner-Galactic Covenant. Such a ship as your own world might launch."

"Umm, I'm going to have to learn more about these Strumbermians," I said. After all, as Minister of—"Hey, watch your—"

But it was too late: already Captain Fuzzpuff had stepped into an apparently empty elevator shaft. He floated there, his head still turned backwards, and beckoned with his six hands for us to join him.

I stepped forward hesitantly.

"Oh, don't be concerned," Fuzzpuff said. "It's a lot like the primitive sport you Earthians call sky-diving."

That did not reassure me particularly, but I

screwed my courage to the sticking point and stepped to the brink.

Chicken!

Qumax's mental ridicule nudged me in. There was no problem. My arms and legs floated and my torso was buoyed as though by water. My shirt fluffed out and so did my pantlegs and, I think, my hair—but that was all. It was enough.

Nancy joined us, and on her the effect was more spectacular. Her hair wafted outward all around her head, and her coveralls nearly ballooned into a baggie. Had she been wearing a skirt ... but I'd better control my obscene thoughts before she learned to read them!

Qumax fried some more bacon.

Nitti distended even more, resembling a bloated pig. But Qumax floated serenely coiled, unchanged. The brat was showing off again.

We swam upward one deck, using limbs or tentacles. It was easy.

"Here we are at the recreation deck," said Captain Fuzzpuff. "After you are officially registered as passengers, you will come here to mingle with the others. There aren't really very many, no more than five or six hundred, since this is a cargo vessel. I trust you will discover suitable entertainments." He looked at his watch—he didn't have a watch, but that was what the gesture suggested—and made his apologies. "I have other business, now, unfortunately. I'm sure one of the seasoned passengers will be happy to show you around, however."

An alien with the winsome countenance of a baby seal slither-slipped close. It extended a flipper to me that miraculously became a webfingered hand. "Corcos Lamorcos?" it inquired politely.

"Not on your slavedriving life!" Qumax exclaimed. "Get out of here, Spevarian!"

The sealoid slid back, looking hurt.

"What an impolite rebuff!" Nancy said angrily. "It's only trying to be friendly."

Qumax indulged in more deep-fat frying. This was a side of him I had not properly appreciated before—the really cruel childish side, that thought it hilarious to insult a sensitive, friendly stranger. "Bring it back," I said. "We'll accept its offer to show us around—if it's still interested."

The captain went to the seal and talked briefly. The two returned. "The Spevarian Bumvelde will be happy to show you around," Fuzzpuff said. "No obligation. He didn't understand."

Qumax sizzled some more, but did not comment. How bratty could you get?

Bumvelde extended his flipper again and I took it. The extremity was so cool as to seem some kind of plant-leaf, yet there was a sensation of hidden warmth coursing through the digits and a gentle pressure of muscles. Then I felt a very careful, very respectful touch in my mind, partly like a caress and partly like three thousand questions simultaneously.

The Spevarian was learning my language.

Then the sensation was gone. "Over there is a fine library," Bumvelde said, pointing to a glassed-in cage.

I gaped. "Already? You know English after only these few seconds?" But I reminded myself that Fuzzpuff had done the same thing.

"No, Harold Prodkins," Bumvelde said. "I merely transposed the configuration of meanings to my own vocabulary, and translate automatically as I go along. This leads to some clumsiness of expression, but not major, I fancy. I think in my own system, and some concepts do not interpolate well."

I let it go at that. He obviously could operate well enough with his system, whatever it was. "That's the library," I said unnecessarily to Nancy.

"Sound, scent, mind tapes and collections of meaningful symbols," Bumvelde said. "Much good literature and much information. I research there regularly."

"Very interesting," I said. "And what is that other area?" I gestured to a sunken place in the floor where aliens of hardly conceivable shape and form gamboled in air.

"The swimming pool. All lifeforms do not appreciate water, but more accept low gravity. You also?"

"I'd probably like it," I agreed. But it seemed to me that I had already experienced low gravity a couple of times—once in the entrance chamber and again in the elevator shaft. Here gravity seemed about normal. Maybe it was like Earthly foibles, where a bath is not the same as a swim. "And over there?" I seemed to be doing all the questioning; the others, even Qumax, merely followed along.

"Entertainment place. Shows, recitals, whatever."

Bumvelde then led the way through the entire recreation area, identifying everything. There was too much; my mind let the new facts slip almost as rapidly as they entered, leaving me with a general impression of wonder. But Nancy, I could tell, was fascinated.

At one point I stumbled against what I took to be a very large hassock. The long ruglike tongue attached to it straightened and looked at me from two brilliant eyeballs on straight eyestalks. Antennae wiggled. A slip of a mouth opened and spoke in a high-pitched sizzle.

"Sorry," I mumbled, amazed. "Accident." Bum-

velde said something incomprehensible to the
creature—relaying my apology, I hoped—and it
settled down again.

We swung around a procession of what seemed
to be otters engrossed in some sort of follow-the-
leader game and impervious to the cares of other
passengers; paused at a stool on which squatted a
huge blue toad with four-finger hands clasping
what was assuredly a newspaper; circled a group
of rowdy raccoon types hoisting big mugs of black
brew in a drinking contest; ducked some oversized, overstuffed birds as they dipped and spi-
raled above a ringed target on which they dropped
darts; and finally emerged behind a deckwall on
the edge of a long court. Here two praying-mantis
characters faced each other across a tennis net.
Each mantis held a long pole in each long-fingered
hand. As we came on the scene each mantis bowed
and the four pole-tips clicked together above the
net.

"Watch," said the Spevarian. "This is a gravbop
contest. Both players are from the Devian system,
where the game is outlawed—as it is most places."

Nancy moved close. "What is it?"

"It's a primitive sport of regrettable popular-
ity," Bumvelde explained. "Originally a Strumbermian combat sport, and as cruel and uncivi-
lized as its inventors."

Strumbermians. They were the raiders I had
heard mentioned before. I had the impression
Bumvelde didn't approve of the game, yet he
watched with a certain fascination. As did we all.

The nearest Devian unrolled a chameleon's tongue
from its mandibled mouth and vibrated its forked
tongue at us. I needed no translation to know that
we'd been treated to an insulting raspberry.

A shrill whistle sounded. I saw a third, a fourth, and a fifth mantis crowded into a box suspended from the deck's ceiling. One of them tossed out a ball of a size midway between that of a baseball and a basketball. It lowered to the nettop, spinning. The players waited, their four poles raised.

Lights flashed from the ceiling. An even number of lighted globes drifted from identical ceiling boxes and moved above the floor on either side of the court. The lights were the same size as the ball.

Another whistle blasted, and both mantis leaped forward and swung their poles.

Four poles came together with a resounding crack. The poles moved apart, swung together. Crack-crack! they went as each player tried to get by the other's guard. The player who was closest feinted with his right pole; the farther Devian blocked. The first brought his left pole around. It collided with the adversary's head. There was a click-clack noise, like that of solarpool balls hitting a vacuum seal. The player fell and the ball zipped after one of the lights.

The ball caught the light, and the light appeared to be ingested by it. The downed opposition player leaped to its feet in quick recovery and batted the ball. The other Devian blocked. Back and forth went the ball, with both players taking long leaps. When a light was bumped by either player or pole, nothing happened. The lights vanished only when there was ball-to-light contact.

"The object of this so-called sport," Bumvelde explained, "is for one player to put out all the opposing player's tag-lights. As you see, each light carries a charge opposite to the gravite on that side of the court. The result is random motion and a seldom-still target. Great skill is required for this barbaric game. And a dense skull."

One player reached a pole across the net in an undisguised attempt to brain his adversary. "Isn't that a foul?" Nancy asked.

"In gravbop," the Spevarian said heavily, "there are very few fouls."

"I'd think they'd need a rest soon," I said, becoming more interested. This was a little like Solarpool, I was thinking. Not the head-bopping, but the light-tagging.

"Rest!" Qumax said, and hissed. I was becoming accustomed to his laughter, but still didn't like it.

"You mean no fouls and no rest periods either?" Nitti asked. This was the first time he'd spoken since we entered the ship. I wondered what was going on in his mind. Alas, I lacked the ability to explore it. Probably, though, he had a pretty good notion of the situation by now.

"None," the sealoid said. "The game is competition carried to its ultimate. Free enterprise without any saving graces."

Watching the Devians, I could believe it. A great sport for capitalists. Properly controlled it might even replace war—killing and all.

"I'll have to set up a court in Lucifernia," Nitti said. He would.

"Do you enjoy gravbop?" the Spevarian asked. "You have a gravbop body. You have long limbs and strong muscles."

"It's hard to enjoy anything so savage," I said, knowing that I *did* rather like it. And I could tell from Nitti's attitude that he was enjoying the spectacle thoroughly. He probably really *would* set up a prison-court. The sadist.

"You'd get your primitive primate head bopped, Harold," Qumax said, with that ubiquitous sizzle.

I took my eyes off the court to glare at him, and in that moment the farther Devian was laid low, probably by a fast-ball shot from his opponent. As the victim fell, the assailant rushed the net and reached across with the pole. It sneaked the ball back, took careful aim and batted out another of its adversary's tag-lights. Considering the game's lack of sportsmanship, this was excellent strategy.

Nancy grabbed my arm, concerned for any injury to anyone or anything. "Is it—is it hurt?"

"Probably," Bumvelde said. "However, heads do heal sometimes, which is more than can be said for the brains of confirmed players."

Nancy looked sick. "I—I don't care for this at all," she confessed. "I want to leave—right now, before these so-called sportsmen manage to exterminate each other."

"But it's just getting interesting," Nitti said. The blood-thirsty turkey! Yet I was loath to leave the game myself.

Nancy started off on her own, and I had to follow. The others hurried to catch up.

"Would you like to stop at the dining salon?" Bumvelde asked.

"Yes!" Nancy and Nitti and I cried almost together. I had not realized it in the continuing novelty and action, but I had never stopped being hungry after the Jupegas sleep. Nancy must have felt the same, and evidently Nitti was just as eager. We all needed to eat.

Bumvelde showed the way to stalls that reminded me of a stable. The smell was not far off, either. I realized that the alien tastes were reflected in the ambient odors; naturally not all were appealing to the human nostril.

"You step in and don a helmet," Bumvelde explained, "and you imagine the food you want, the flavors you desire, and the approximate vitamin and mineral content."

"That'll be tough," I said.

"Not really. I'm sure we have a record of what is
needed for humanoid nutrition. The food will taste
strange at first, as it must, because it is a synthe-
sis. But a little practice and you'll become expert.
Don't worry about wasting it; the scraps are all
reprocessed."

I wished he hadn't mentioned that last detail.
How many reprocessed alien scraps would *my* meal
be composed of? "I doubt I'll be much of an expert," I said gloomily. This was like dancing for
my dinner—and I wasn't much of a showman.

I looked over the booths. No sense in taking one
of the large ones that seemed designed for a creature with a giraffe's neck. Or one of the squirrel-
roost ones. Or the one that resembled a flooded
hog-wallow. There were several booths of the appropriate size and complexion. Nancy and I stepped
into one.

"Nancy," I said, "you're the doctor. Suppose
you order for us?"

"Right away, boss," she said, lifting the shining
helmet. We waited there at the counter. Perspira-
tion beaded her face. Nothing else happened.

"I'm afraid I'm too inhibited," she said sheepishly.

"Here, let me," I said. I should have realized
that with her mind-block she would not get through.
I took over the helmet. I thought of a delicious meal
of filet mignon, pâté de foi gras, heart of artichoke
salad, French pastry, Arabic coffee and rare Span-
ish wines. I made an order for three, knowing Nitti
had to eat too.

The panel burbled. A section of counter lowered.
I took off the helmet.

Nancy waited expectantly. I knew she'd be
surprised.

The top of the counter let out a ping. There were three trays. I closed my eyes blissfully and sniffed.

I inhaled the stench of bloated corpses drifting in a hot sewer.

I opened my eyes.

I shut them again. "Can't get it perfect every time," I mumbled.

"Harold," Nancy said, holding a handkerchief to her face with one hand while she delicately nudged the first tray toward the disposal slot, "perhaps something simpler?"

"Um." I might have said more, but that would have required breathing, and the fumes were too strong. I took up the helmet.

This time I thought very carefully of simple foods, omitting the side thoughts that had messed me up. Those fancy dressings and sauces and wines were not so delectable for my plebeian tastes even when they were right. This time I strove for naturality.

We looked at the trays. The colors were right and so were the shapes. I picked up my hot dog and bit tentatively at one end. It was edible.

"You forgot the mustard," Nancy said.

I ignored her and stepped around to the next booth to notify Nitti that his meal was ready. And stopped.

Nitti was well into a platter of filet mignon, and had an entire decanter of rare French wine. Plus trimmings.

I should have known he'd be a successful gourmet.

"Perhaps it is time I show you to your quarters," Bumvelde said after we had dined.

Swimming downdeck was no harder than swimming updeck. As we emerged onto the landing we were met by three female Prunians—those with the monkey faces and the built-in bra-padding. They were on their way up and they stopped their chattering long enough to produce sharp-toothed smiles. I wanted irrationally to return the gesture, but found it impossible to look at them. Shame, though a natural part of Earthly existence, now interfered with my reactions.

"Those Prunians," Bumvelde said, "are a very primitive species."

"I can see that," I said. I wanted, nevertheless, to look back up the shaft. At least one part of me did. From this vantage the anatomy under those short, so-human (prior to the baggie fashion) skirts would be rather clearly visible . . .

Go ahead. Peek! And a mental frying sound. Damn Qumax!

"Do you feel well?" Nancy asked solicitously. "You look flushed."

"Must be tired," I lied.

"Here's a stateroom for you Earthians," Bumvelde said as we came down a level hall. He stopped at a door and opened it. I stared inside at what appeared to be almost human furniture.

"We can synthesize any furnishings you design for yourselves," the Spevarian said. "Robot tailors will also provide you with whatever you desire in the way of body coverings. I must warn you that it is not wise to go about the ship without body-coverings or to defecate anywhere except in a lavatory. Some individuals are amazingly sensitive about natural functions."

I looked at Nancy. She was upset about something. Then I realized. "We can't all stay in one room," I said.

"Prince Qumax has a separate compartment, naturally."

"No! I mean—there are human-human sensibilities that—the three of us are different. That is, two of us are—" I stopped and bit my lip. Damn! I didn't want to share a room with Nitti and I was reasonably certain Nancy was not about to share with either of us.

"What he's trying to say," Nancy put in, "is that we each want separate rooms."

"Each?" The little seal seemed astonished.

"Each."

"But I'm afraid that's impossible. There is only one room at the moment suitable for humanoids. I can ask the captain—"

"You could install suitable partitions," Nitti said.

A prison warden would naturally think of that, I thought resentfully. But it did seem feasible.

Soon a tribe of carpenter-robots appeared and went to work.

"Shall we now discuss corcos Lamorcos?" Bumvelde inquired hopefully.

"No!" Qumax said immediately. "We told you we weren't interested."

Again the selfish brat, I thought. This Bumvelde had been perfectly decent to us, using up his own time to show us around, and now he wanted to talk about whatever-it-was. Why not?

"I'll talk with you," Nancy said. "Let's go for a walk while these gentlemen supervise the carpenters." And she departed with the seal.

Good for her, I decided.

"She'll be sorry," Qumax said, and hissed hilariously.

"Oh? Why?" I was curious. Even brats had their reasons for their attitudes.

"Don't you know what corcos Lamorcos *is?*"

"Of course I don't know! We just came aboard, remember? And you never let Bumvelde explain."

"We've been aboard a few hours, by your reckoning," he said smugly, rumpling a section of his torso. "But at our velocity, that's about a thousand light years distance. In another day we'll be at Jamborango."

"A thousand light years!" My mind balked at the notion. "I didn't know we were even out of the Solar system!"

"What," asked Nitti, who had kept his mind on the main subject, "is corcos Lamorcos?"

"A slave contract," Qumax said, and went into a convulsion of frying.

～～～ Chapter 8 ～～～

I started down the passageway, determined to find Nancy and warn her before it was too late. Behind me the worm's obnoxious merriment mingled with the chuckles of Warden Nitti.

I got lost, of course. I ran up and down halls calling for her, attracting curious glances from pedestrians. A curious glance from a creature with three or four long-stalked eyeballs is something, but I couldn't give up. No luck.

I finally made my disgruntled way back toward the cabins. As I sulked down the passage I was almost bowled over by the huge snail we had seen in the recreation area. It slid by without so much as a thought for me, intent on getting somewhere fast. And it *was* fast, despite the large shell. It was as though it was sliding down a polished chute, except that this track was level. There was no trail of smear behind it, either. The eye-stalks rolled wildly as it passed.

Down the hall a door slammed. One of the three Prunians ran by. She went on simian tip-toe, her newborn-baby face wrinkling with emotion. Her monkey-tail swished fleetingly. What was going on?

And there before our cabin were Nancy and Bumvelde. They had come back while I careened about the ship. "Nancy!" I cried. "I have to warn you—"

"Yes, we just heard," she said, her face flushed with excitement.

"You didn't sign anything? Make any irrevocable contracts?"

She looked at me questioningly.

"Corcos Lamorcos," I said. "It's slavery. You mustn't—"

"Oh, Harold," she said, irritated.

"He hasn't heard," Nitti said.

"Heard what? Am I too late?"

"Harold, a strange ship had been detected following us," Nancy said. "They say it could be a Strumbermian raider."

That *was* new. "But they don't attack registered ships," I pointed out.

"They *usually* don't," Qumax said. Even he looked worried.

There was a blackening.

I found myself on the floor in the dark, one hand grasping Nancy's arm. I was terrified. I heard noises all around us, and each jarred as though a spike was being hammered against my skull. Phantasms of utter horror gaped at me. "Nancy!" I cried.

Then the lights came on again. We were strewn all along the hall. Yet I had felt no crash.

"Psychological attack," Bumvelde said, picking himself up. "Strumbermian tactic. Demoralize everyone, then board—"

It struck again. Formless things of nightmare swooped and pounced, and the pain of their scratches and bites and stings and burns was real. This time I realized that the lights had not failed; I had merely clamped my eyes shut in my terror and fallen to the floor. I pried them open. Nancy, beside me, was writhing with her hands clapped to her face. And my fear lessened, for she needed comforting.

I flung my arms about her, pulling her tight to me. "I love you!" I cried in her ear.

The siege abated. Nancy opened her eyes. "What did you say?"

I found myself speechless. I had not known I would say those words, and wasn't certain now that I meant them. And they seemed silly, with the fear-wave gone.

The floor shook. A shape loomed in the hall.

"Strumbermian!" Bumvelde cried. "They boarded!"

SILENCE! It was the mental blast of the pirate coming at us. Pale and grossly humanoid, the thing was an appalling caricature of Dr. Frankenstein's creation. It aimed one huge extremity at Nancy and me. *COME, EARTH-THINGS!*

I looked at Nancy—not over one hundred thirty pounds, and this Strumbermian a bad five hundred. Her judo would be useless here. "I—"

EARTH-THINGS NOT COMMUNICATE!

I looked at the pointing finger, the size of my arm. I decided not to communicate. Taking Nancy's tender hand, I followed the Strumbermian's broad, broad back. We filed up the corridor. Behind us, meekly, came Nitti and Qumax.

We marched—down through nightmare. Screams, mental and physical, came at us from every side. Flesh was burning somewhere. One stateroom had its door torn off; inside, on the wide sleeping pallet, one of the baby-faced Prunians had her hairy

arms locked about the throat of a Strumbermian.
The monster had her by the tail, his massive thumb
poking up under it. The other hand was yanking
her skirt off. Then we were by, to see the other
rooms, other atrocities in progress. In the salon we
saw the snail-creature, his shell smashed, his body
twitching and oozing ichor.

I tried to look at Nancy, to reassure her. I
couldn't. Nitti and Qumax had disappeared.

We went through the airlock and stopped in the
anteroom. Here lay the wrecked remains of Nitti's
copter (not that it was much use in deep space),
and broken spider robots were piled with mangled
alien bodies. We waited for an interminable period amid the carnage, not daring to speak. Then
at last we were directed past the wreckages and
the dead, stopping at a huge transparent tube that
joined our ship's entry port to the facing hatch of a
long, black starship.

I saw lines of spider robots carrying tremendous
loads from the cargo hold. There were boxes, bales,
crates, kegs—all sorts of cargo. I wondered what it
was these robots carried that was so valuable it
had to be transferred piecemeal. Why did any of it
have to be moved at all, if the *Comet's Tail* had
been fully secured by the pirates? It would be
easier to take the entire ship to port and unload
there.

"Over here, Minister!"

I looked. It was Nitti, calling and motioning at
me. A Strumbermian with a star branded on its
forehead stood glowering beside him. I looked at
Nancy, not comprehending.

"You're to come with me, Minister," the warden
said.

I stood there uncertainly. "But—"

GO, EARTH-THING!

I looked at the brute who seemed to have made the order. "I don't understand."

GO! That two-by-four finger leveled at me.

Hardly knowing what I was doing, I stepped over to where Nitti was waiting. "What's this all about, Warden?"

"We're going back inside the *Comet's Tail.* They're going to turn it loose, after it's gutted."

"But—" I looked back where Nancy stood like a doll beside the towering Strumbermian. "Nancy—Qumax—"

And suddenly I got it.

Warden Nitti had made a deal of some kind. A deal with the pirates. For his life and my life. Only.

"I'll kill you!" I cried, and meant it.

"No. You don't understand. I—I would have been all alone. One human is all they need. One Earthian to question. They'd rather have one bound over by majority vote—that makes it legal, by galactic law—and since you're the Minister—"

I threw myself at him. I grabbed a handful of shirt, chopped a knuckle at his fat throat. . . .

And fell on my face before doing any damage. It was as though I had been electrocuted.

"I tried," I heard him say. "Now they'll just take both of you. They don't care *that* much about the law." When the haze of pain cleared he was nearly at the far end of the airlock saving himself while he could. Nancy was crying, and Qumax—

Qumax was starting across that damnably solid transparent connecting tube, tentacles drooping in utter defeat.

Beyond the end of the tube I saw into the Strumbermian raider. I marched back to Nancy, grabbed her hand, and led her into the tube. If we were to be taken captive, we'd go with our heads up, not whimpering like baby worms.

Stars whirled outside, underfoot. I could not look at them and keep my balance in the trace gravity. Whichever way I peered, I felt as though I should fall on my head. I did not want to rivet my gaze to Nancy. Or Qumax. And certainly not the Strumbermians. But man is not made to tread empty space.

Gravite-coated metal came under my feet at last. I looked at my companions. Nancy had stopped crying, and was now the chin-up, determinedly brave extraterrestrialogist. Qumax remained the child—antennae dropping, muzzle averted, the very picture of hopelessness. That, I realized, was the essential difference between the child and the adult, whatever the abilities or intelligence or cultural status: the manner he stood up under stress. The child gave up; the adult carried on.

We were marched through corridors swarming with red ratlike things that I presumed had some function other than vermin business, to an unesthetic version of the stateroom we had never quite used. Our captors shoved us inside, closed and locked the door, and left. We were alone—for how long?

Almost alone. Nancy flinched as a rat—actually a grotesque flesh-thing resembling a rodent—scooted from the lavatory recess. Without thinking I put my arm around her.

"Harold, you're a fool," she said. "You could have gone with Nitti. You should have!" But she didn't move away. "You've your mission to think about. To make Jamborango apologize. To win respect for Earth. Instead of that, you—you—"

"Shut up, Nancy," I said, and kissed her one.

It was such an unexpected move on my part that it amazed us both.

"You did mean it," she murmured, and I knew she was thinking of my declaration of love during the fear-siege.

"It isn't over yet!" Qumax exclaimed, suddenly enthusiastic. Of all the times to interrupt!

The great worm lay at the port window. His antennae stuck out like horns and his skin rumpled reflexively. He was staring at the place where the connecting tube joined the *Comet's Tail*. We joined him and peered out.

A battle was going on inside the *Comet's Tail*'s docking chamber, which remained held open by the connecting tube between ships. Somehow the entire section remained sealed, so that the vacuum of space did not intrude. The freight handlers of the two vessels were fighting each other—grappling, striking, tearing—in mindless arachnid fury.

But why hadn't the *Comet's Tail*'s equipment rallied to its defense before? I decided that the shock and surprise of the Strum attack must have disorganized the supervisory personnel, so that no effective action had been possible. Now enough time had passed for the cargo ship to rally its crew, and things were happening. It seemed backwards—first the conquest, then the battle—but feasible.

People were also becoming involved. I thought of them as people, though in fact they were all manner of alien creatures. A Strum officer with a star on his forehead lay dead near the tube's end. Other Strums were trying to get in shots with their weapons. But there were few of them. Probably too many had indulged in victorious debaucheries, so that the raider's force had been dispersed and dissipated. Bad tactics, I thought; they should have been *sure* the prey was secure before running rampant.

Broken cargo strewed the lock. At the far end a trio of defenders appeared wearing spacesuits. Ahead of these crawled two robots holding a tall transparent shield. In the center position behind that shield strode the three-foot Captain Fuzzpuff, flanked by two tall Devians.

A Strumbermian officer gestured. Something like a machinegun went into action; I couldn't see it because of the angle, but I saw the broken beam of its firing. Curling white vapor struck the barrier and played with livid fury. A glowing area formed in front of Fuzzpuff.

The captain took up a weapon at a shield-port, aimed down its barrel and fired. He and the gun jerked as though from recoil, but I saw no projectile and heard no sound. A Strum dropped. The party pressed forward.

More Strums appeared. They must, I thought, have been piling out from the black ship. Now there were at least twenty opposed to the three defenders and two robot shield-carriers. Four to one odds, whichever way you looked at it.

Strumbermians blasted at the advancing shield, and it showed white where struck. At the shield's weapon-port Fuzzpuff fired bolts of blue incandescence now, picking off enemy robots.

But there were too many raiders. From behind the ruined copter two Strums sent a heavy freight-handler. Arachnid legs carried the mechanical creature up and over one of the falling packing cases. It dropped in front of the shield, raised dull black forelegs and began striking the barrier.

The transparency dented. In vain did Captain Fuzzpuff attempt to align his weapon. Other robots charged.

The Devian at the captain's right opened a higher weapon-port. Aiming point-blank, it released a deep purple blast. The freight-handler dropped, lay still, turned dark gray and dissolved at last into a lead-colored powder. The shield advanced over the dust. But even as it did, two more robots leaped barriers to ram pointed forelegs into the open muzzles of the defender's weapons. Unlike the carrying mechanisms, these robots were equipped with red glowing axes. The Strums had probably adapted them specially for this sort of closework. They wrestled the gun muzzles aside and raised the axes.

I gripped Nancy's hand. It was horrible to be so helpless. If only I could be out there helping, doing something—if only I hadn't been so ready to capitulate myself—

But at the same time I knew that my ignorance would already have killed me—and Nancy—ten times over out there. The best way I could help was to stay well out of the way—as I was doing. Still, I did not feel proud.

From the *Comet's Tail*'s inner lock came another defender. It wore a tall, tall spacesuit and could only be one of the giraffe-necked passengers I had seen.

Axes split the shield. Captain Fuzzpuff and the Devians leaped back, but not Giraffe-Neck. Clutching something oblong that it suddenly pushed forward, it leaped with long, ungainly strides for the rent in the barrier.

Giraffe-Neck hit the shield and there was an explosion. Bits of flesh, metal and other debris shot outward. As the smoke cleared Captain Fuzzpuff and one Devian were all I could see moving among the shambles. The Devian had one arm twisted, another missing.

Getting to his feet, the tough little beetle-captain grabbed an ax from the disintegrated limb of a robot. He scuttled to the connecting tube. The Devian followed, shooting bursts of blue ahead of the captain.

Strumbermians fell like monster weeds before a scythe, but continued to charge the Pmpermian. Fuzzpuff would not be stopped. At the end of his mad charge he braced himself on short, wide-spread insect-legs, raised his ax and brought it down again and again upon the end of the transparent shaft where it bonded to the open port.

"He's trying to chop it through!" Nancy whispered.

So he was. At first nothing happened. Then the area of his blows took on a light copper tinge. Slowly the color deepened from deep brass to apricot.

Then, with a visible explosion of released air, the *Comet's Tail* parted its dreadful company with the Strumbermian raider. The entire end of the tube shattered, and I saw robots, bodies and other objects sucked out from both locks to spray into the vacuum between the ships.

We were stranded.

Chapter 9

THERE were stars outside our port. The near ones passed rapidly behind, the far ones seemed hardly to move. I was reminded of land features as seen from a speeding car: perspective made things nearest at hand seem to pass most swiftly. Here it reinforced the three-dimensional effect; the view was phenomenally impressive.

But one of the stars was moving out of phase with the others. It blinked on and off like a spaceborne traffic light, and I wondered about brave Captain Fuzzpuff and the Devian and the open airlock. . . .

A larger dot came into view; then a row of dots rotated into evidence. No stars—those lights represented the *Comet's Tail!* I had thought it was gone, but it was traveling alongside of the pirate, since the Strums had matched velocities for the raid. Now the cargo vessel was falling behind, crippled, losing the phase. The lights blurred, became a Solarpool comet in an infinitely expanded gametable, dwindled and were gone.

Nancy sighed. "I hope all those heroics weren't in vain. I hope those spacesuits. . . . "

"The captain and the Devian will have gotten inside," Qumax said almost confidently. "But they could have saved themselves the trouble. Did you see the way that tube shattered? The Strums were starting to accelerate without drawing in the umbilical cord. It would have cracked off anyway in a few more moments, under that stress."

Nancy trembled. "All those poor crewmen. W-will the Strumbermians blow up the *Comet's Tail*?"

"No. They might like to, since they're outlaws and killers, but if they violate the code of space that blatantly they'll have the entire space force down on them, and that would be the end."

"Isn't pirating a ship in high space a crime?" Nancy asked.

"Not enough of one to warrant full-scale action. Oh, there'll be a couple more police ships assigned to this locale, and the Strums will feel the pinch. But nothing like the pinch they'd feel if they wiped out an entire cargo ship. So they—"

Something slammed us. I was thrown to the floor along with Nancy and Qumax. Lying on my side, I saw a bright green dart flash by the port. I knew that this was a strange vessel and that our ship was being fired on.

"Galactic police ship already!" Qumax cried. "No wonder the Strums started moving out so fast. We're saved, if we're not destroyed along with the raiders."

"They wouldn't shoot down a ship with hostages aboard," I said, somewhat feebly.

"They don't know I'm aboard, and you don't count," Qumax said. He didn't seem very happy.

I wasn't very happy either. I hoped the raider would not be blasted out of space while we were aboard, but I didn't see much future for us if it escaped, either.

The ship shivered and shrugged. Overwhelming disorientation took hold. I imagined I was lying on the floor with my feet over my head. I *was!* I looked at the others. Qumax, poor worm, was rolled into something resembling a green pool ball, bouncing this way and that. Nancy was fortunate to be wearing coveralls, though these were beginning to tear again. Her heels, like mine, seemed directed ceiling-ward.

"That's a police cruiser all right," Qumax said. "Probably the latest equipment aboard. New tracking stuff. If they can get locked on and . . ."

WHAM! I thought my insides were splashed all over the Strumbermian stateroom. They weren't. Too bad. It would have been simpler.

"Were the police keeping an eye on the *Comet's Tail*?" Nancy asked. "Maybe they *do* know about you. . . ."

A ball bounced and Qumax's face emerged. "Farewell, Harold Prodkins! Farewell, Nancy Dilsmore! Farewell. Farewell, Captain Fuzzpuff. Farewell, Swarm Tyrant. Farewell, life—"

"Qumax! For Heaven's sake!" said Nancy.

"I hear them coming," Qumax said in direful tones. Big tears formed in his eyes.

"Can't you use your power to control them one at a time, send them away?" I asked. "If you were able to break us out of Lucifernia—"

"Not the Strums! They have awful minds!"

Heavy footsteps thumped up to our door and stopped. I didn't dare discuss escape with Qumax now, even if the worm had the spine for it, which he didn't.

The door crashed open. Facing us were three

stony-faced Strumbermians, one an officer with a star branded on his forehead.

The huge finger of the officer pointed. First to me, then Qumax. *COME! CONTROL ROOM!*

I pushed my feet off the wall and got my legs under me. Groggily I stood. I looked at the blank porthole, then at Nancy.

NOW! the Strum ordered mind-deafeningly.

"Nancy," I cried. "Remember, death before dis—"

YOU DEFY ME, MOBILE-FACED CREATURE?! A quarter ton of meat-muscle loomed over me.

I had a vision of a smokey medieval hell, the devil challenging me. *I defy you!* I thought. *You and all your ilk! I—*

It seemed that a large ax split my skull and drove downward to the crotch, leaving me twain. Streaks of red exploded outward from my eyeballs. I was picked up and shaken until my teeth fell out and splatted against the deck like hailstones. I had the impression of dirt rammed up my nostrils and packed by the shovelful into my ears. There were rat-snouts and rat-squeals and rat scurryings, outside or inside of my skull.

Whatever held me dropped my feet. I was yanked to a standing position and jerked around to face whatever my handler had it in mind for me to face. My teeth, it developed, were still in my mouth and my body was intact, but my eyesight was not so good yet. There *was* some dirt in my ear.

Something flickered like the image on a mistuned trebvee set. Something like a face on Mt. Rushmore, or maybe a posterior—but the features were all haze to me.

Things began, unfortunately, to clear. I saw silhouettes in a fog of my mind's own making. There were Strumbermians and there was Qumax. I tried in vain to distinguish the trebvee image. Qumax was speaking to it, begging it, wheedling it in a strange tone and language.

Something the size of a rat zipped across the floor. A big Strum foot came up, and down. There was a ratlike squeal and spray of red. Qumax started and knocked against the trebvee. The set blinked and the image changed to a confusing light-pattern.

Reacting as to a blow, Qumax jerked away. He careened into a control bank. A Strumbermian roared mentally and started for him. Qumax screeched as the rat had screeched, and rumpled farther into the nest of gauges, levers and controls. His tentacles leaped about at random—pulling, turning, jerking. Click, snap, zap.

Then several bright flashes amid the alien instruments, and a light like an aerial-display firework.

Something slammed me.

Agony. Floor. Qumax's mind screams.

From a pain-shot void came the sweetest words I'd heard in at least an eternity. They lanced in at me, tickled my consciousness, and finally registered intelligence. "Harold, oh, Harold—why did you have to be such a fool?"

I forced blistered eyelids open and saw the face of Nancy Dilsmore. She was looking down at me from no more than two feet away. I saw beauty in those features and I found that the tears on those smooth cheeks were infinitely precious to me. I wondered . . . and then I began remembering.

"Harold, oh, Harold. You poor, poor fool, Harold."

Never before had such precious, original words come to me. "Nancy," I grunted eloquently.

Blue eyes blinked. A drop hung on her nose until she raised an ungloved hand to brush it off. "You should have known better than to start trouble," she said.

"*I* start trouble?"

"In the control room. You and Qumax."

"I—" Had there been a mind-itch in the middle of that session? I didn't even know why we had been taken there. Probably only to broadcast our pictures to Jamborango, so that the Swarm Tyrant would have to pay ransom. But Qumax had fouled it up by his tantrum . . . No, let her think it was I. "What—what about Qumax?"

"He—he's in the lavatory," she said.

Sure enough, I saw his tail. It was limp. "Badly hurt?"

"Not too badly. Nothing permanent, I think. His face is swollen and he has some ugly bruises, but otherwise—"

"Otherwise still the ornery worm," I said unkindly. "How about you?" I hated myself for saying it, but knew I had to ask.

"Me?"

"While we were gone."

"Ohhh . . . nothing," she said.

Was she lying? Probably. Yet there were no bruises, no scratches, no blood, no sundered coveralls. She had even repatched the rips from the capture and transfer. She was claiming that she had not been molested—yet how could I be sure, after that Prunian episode I had seen?

"They didn't," she said. "Really."

I sat up. I was sure then that this was true. She really would have died first. I took her in my arms. I kissed her lips. I felt Qumax's scratchiness.

Angry, I looked around to see the worm, one eye closed, antenna drooping. Obviously he was playing possum, listening in on my mental processes and ready to make me do something at an inopportune moment. I wondered how I could enforce privacy. I glanced again at Nancy and knew that she was seeing Qumax and guessing about the scratchiness. There was no privacy for such as us, not under these circumstances.

And I knew she'd rather die than do anything with that kind of publicity.

"They're coming again, Harold Prodkins!"

Qumax's agonized warning caught me staring at the stars. We had come out of hyperspace, or whatever it was. The raider had long since lost the cruiser. Either the police had realized who was aboard and had to desist, or they had not been very good hunters.

The worm was cringing again. He certainly lost his obnoxious composure in the presence of these Strums!

I looked once more at Nancy, regretting what had not passed between us. Her golden hair, her unbagged form, her smile—I wanted to photograph it all in my memory. Before—

With chilling abruptness the door flew back. In strode the Strumbermian with the red star burned into the waxy flesh of his flat expanse of forehead. Straight to me he walked, stopped, pointed that finger and thought: *COME!* Evidently these creatures never communicated in less than a blast.

"Harold—"

"Good-bye Nancy," I said. I stood up rapidly to make the parting easier.

Once more tears stood in her eyes. "You be careful, Harold."

I tried to say something manly, but got choked up. The Strum officer nudged me with a mountainous hand and I stumbled ignominiously out. That was my noble leavetaking. I hadn't even asked Qumax to look out for her, though that would have done little good anyway. When the brat wasn't making mischief, he was cowering abjectly.

We marched down the unadorned, rat-infested corridors again. At one intersection I saw the food troughs—metal dikes filled with flowing, greasy meal-synthetic that reminded me of hog slop. We had been offered a bucketful, but hadn't touched it.

I was boosted into a large, luxurious office, free of rats. The door slammed behind me.

Another Strumbermian officer peered at me through eyes that were even deader than most Strum orbs. The star on his forehead was larger and redder than the others I had seen. His skin was even more ghastly pallid. Obviously sunbathing was not popular on Strumbermia. He was sitting on a low stool that kept his knees raised almost to his square hairless chin. He motioned me to a similar stool. *SQUAT!* he thought.

I looked at the stool, waist-high on me and fraught with great splinters. "May I stand?" I asked hesitantly. I couldn't really make things much worse for myself.

SUIT SELF, MOBILE-FACED ONE. The officer's eyes were an unpleasant purple bloodshot despite their deadness. It was as though they had bled and rotted some after expiring. From where he squatted he could gaze directly into my face. I decided to take a seat after all.

YOUR NAME HAROLD PRODKINS, EARTHIAN, telepathed the Strumbermian with the usual power. *YOU REPRESENTATIVE OF YOUR WORLD. I CROG. I BIG SHOT LEADER.* The force of his mind-talk threatened to give me a headache.

"What do you want?" I asked. I felt no bravado; I knew he would get whatever he wanted, whether I resisted or not.

WANT TO KNOW ABOUT EARTH. CLIMATE, NATURAL RESOURCES.

"I'll think about that," I said, meaning it literally. I launched into a mental description of the worst barely habitable planet I had ever read about in science fiction. I conjured a vision of flowing lakes of lava; tried to remember the composition of a corrosive atmosphere hostile to most known life-forms; pictured hothouse cities that moved about the planet on huge off-center rollers that were buffeted here and there by multiple hurricanes. Metallic-based lifeforms with twelve-inch teeth that sucked blood by the quart; unpredictable but frequent and devastating meteoric showers; an unstable orbit that made lava lakes freeze and crack jaggedly every few years, then melt and bubble and flow across the land; horrendous earthquakes and elephant-gobbling pitcher-plants. The national gourmet delicacy that resembled my first attempt to make a synthetic meal aboard the *Comet's Tail*. I was working up some research about the imminence of the sun going nova and the frantic efforts to suppress the bone-crunching sea monsters when Crog reached out and tapped me crushingly with a stonehard finger.

YOU LIE, MOBILE-FACE!

I gasped. Not only had that finger-blow nearly dislocated my ribcage, I had distinctly felt an electric shock.

YOU HUMANOID. HUMANOIDS ALL BRAG ABOUT HOME PLANETS!

So old stoneface didn't swallow it. It had been worth the try, still. Certainly I would not voluntarily tell the truth. "Maybe I'm different," I said.

NO? YOU LIE. YOUR PLANET NOT GOOD AS THAT!

"Not as—" I felt my face hang open.

Crog opened his cavernous mouth in what could have been either a smile or open mockery of my astonishment. His teeth were not human at all—they were sharp and pointed, like those of a tyrannosaur. He leaned forward and almost disabled me with another finger tap.

YOU TRY TO IMPRESS BIG SHOT LEADER. CROG NOT MIND YOU LIE. IMPLIES YOU TRUE HUMANOID.

"True human—" I really had felt the shock this time.

"We speak with sound if you like, now," Crog said, surprising me again. "Now I know you one of us."

"I am?" I couldn't think fast enough to adjust to this.

"You not bug. You not worm or other vermin. You humanoid!"

"I suppose so, that way." Maybe if he stayed out of my thoughts—

"Very good!" Crog agreed. "You realize that Strumbermians and Earthians have common interest; try to impress Crog how much courage you have and how much help you be. Now I not have to use mind-probe."

"You're very smart," I lied. Mind-probe—ugh! I could guess what that would do to my brain-tissue.

"We need planet like this. Plenty metals, plenty protected from invasion. You know, describe perfectly."

"Yes," I said cautiously. Was this hulk playing cat-and-mouse with me?

"Now Strumbermians and Earthians be allies."

"Well . . ." Here it comes, I thought. I tried hard to blank out my genuine sentiments. Apparently the Strums didn't pick up anything that wasn't directed to them, except for vocabulary. I

could test that by thinking a compliment at him
that I knew to be phony ... but I was afraid to
chance it. Right now, anyway.

"You know history? You know how worms and
bugs and vermin get all good planets, keep humanoids out? You know why all humanoids need
fight against ilk?"

"Uh, not very well, I'm afraid."

"True, you newcomer to space. Probably learn
all lies from bugs and worms. Crog tell from
Strumbermian viewpoint. Solid brassplated truth.
You want to hear, Harold Prodkins?"

"Very much," I said. I *was* curious, though hardly
in sympathy. And the longer I could keep him
talking, the more likely there would be time for
the police—*lousy wormbug flatfoots! Hate them!* I
thought desperately, trying to cover my mental
slip.

Crog rose from his stool and crossed to a cabinet. Had he caught on? *Handsome Strumbermian!*
Or was handsomeness considered effeminate? *Strong
humanoid!* I'd better keep my mind buttoned, or
I'd get myself in trouble sure.

From the cabinet he took a container that looked
very much like a wine bottle. Beside the bottle he
set two things that could have been dirty soup
bowls.

I watched with mingled interest and apprehen-
sion as Crog slopped a milky fluid from the bottle
into the bowls. It was a big bottle—a gallon at
least—though it looked small in his hand. The
bowls were, literally, pint-sized. Something told
me I wasn't going to like this. A pint of rotgut ...

Crog returned with the bowls and handed me
one. I peered into it, hoping that I could somehow
avoid imbibing the stuff. An insectoid vaguely like
a flea scooted along the rim and stopped to insert

its proboscis into the brimming liquid. Then it stiffened, jerked its legs about convulsively, and fell in. I fished it out with my finger, afraid it might dissolve.

Crog squatted on his stool again. His bowl went to his lipless mouth, his head tipped back, and the liquid gurgled down like water draining from a spent bathtub. The noise may have signified manners, or plain gusto.

He lowered the bowl, now a quarter empty. "Ah, that good scrotch!" he said. And emitted a belch like a foghorn blast. "You glug."

Under his watchful gaze I raised my own bowl and hesitantly sipped from it. With any luck at all, it would prove as poisonous to me as to that flea . . .

The taste was worse than anything I had been willing to imagine. Rotted pig-mash and fermented nettles might have been the base, not to mention year-old toad urine. My nostrils had not been assailed by such an aroma since—well, that food-synthesis attempt, again.

I lowered the bowl, hacking as the nettles ground into my esophagus. Through streaming eyes I saw Crog nodding wisely at me.

"You get used to it," he said. "You like. All humanoids like. Just wait until effects hit you."

"Effects?" I coughed. So it *was* dope.

"Enjoyable. Like your liqueurs, your pot."

"Oh." Then: "How—?"

"Your Warden Nitti tell us about such things, when he try to make deal. He sensible humanoid."

Ugh, I thought, but did not communicate.

"You glug your scrotch," Crog advised, "and while you glugging it. Crog tell history of Galaxy. Later"—his puffy left eyelid dropped while the rest of his face remained motionless—"Crog have other pleasant surprise for you."

Thought of what Crog might consider pleasant caused me to raise my bowl and glug. Much of my tongue and palate had been anesthetized by the first sip, so it didn't burn so badly this time. Crog glugged noisily after me.

I lowered the bowl and waited for the promised effects. I stared at Crog, clear-headed as space, and realized that he was talking; that he had been for some time.

". . . perfect planet for colony. Few ant hills only sign of life. Fairminded person—you, Harold Prodkins—would say we Strumbermians had right to colonize. What's to stop us—few billion ants? Ants not people. You agree we have right?"

"I, ah, suppose if this world had not been previously claimed by anyone—wasn't on any star maps or included in somebody's territory—"

"It wasn't!" Crog said, slamming his fist on his knee with the sound of an explosion. "It all alone in space, just waiting for humanoid colonists."

"Then I'd say you had a right," I said. Maybe the Strums did have a claim or two. Immediately I felt ashamed of myself for imagining it. These were pirates!

"Glad you agree," said Crog. "As say, only ant heaps. So Strum troops move in with armored vehicles to set up colony."

"But I thought you said the place was uninhabited!"

"Was so. Only ants. Big ants."

"Oh!" Now I got the picture. Big ugly ants like those I used to see on my uncle's farm. God, but I had hated them! I'd poured coal oil on their hills and then set fire to the works.

"Ants very unintelligent. All they have for protection is old atomic cannon and laser rays. Strumbermians cut down all ants without first invitation to gravbop. Why not? They only bugs and not humanoids. We start pull down ant hills, set up cities. Then, we all but win planet, Jamborangs and Imbibels come."

"What'd they do?" Helped the poor deserving humanoids, I hoped.

"Attacked us. *Us!* Chased us off. Claimed planet belong to ants. Claimed we violate their right to free existence—that we must pay damages and agree not to take planet again."

"You fought?" Who would not have fought against such injustice? I wondered.

"No," Crog said regretfully. "Jamborangs and Imbibels too powerful; only fight real wars. Not observe civilized custom of gravbop. We agree leave ants that planet. Not very good planet anyway. We pay for damages, but then"—Crog glugged his scrotch—"then ants invade *us!*"

I glugged my own scrotch. "Terrible," I said, not certain whether I meant ants or drink. "Terrible, terrible, terrible!"

"Jamborangs and Imbibels come back. They see fighting—go to aid of ants again! Aid ants against Strumbermians!"

"The dirty bugs!" I exclaimed, shocked. "Give one a light-year and it'll take a parsec!"

"Strums lose home planet. Lose three, four dozen home planets. Then Strumbermians move into space. Become what called outlaws. But when we grow strong again, we come back to center of galaxy! Enlist aid of all humanoid species! We take back lost planets! Make bugs and worms the outlaws."

What a success story! "Can't say I blame you," I said. "If I'd been there, I'd have been on *your* side. I'd have wanted to stamp the ants out. You bet!"

"I thought you'd say that, Harold Prodkins. Once

you know the truth, not worm-lies. Now you contact your world for us. Make arrangements for Earthians to unite with Strums."

"We-e-ell," I said. It was all so logical; why did I hesitate?

"What you say, Harold Prodkins, Representative of Earth?"

I thought deeply, trying to find a reason against it. "Earth is new on the galactic scene," I said at last. "Doesn't know the bugs from the humanoids."

"You fix, Harold Prodkins?" Crog was pathetically eager.

"Perhaps," I said, my head swimming. Now was no time to make decisions, I realized. But I'd not forgotten that Crog and I had glugged together.

"When you land on Strum planet, you fix," Crog repeated. "That not long now."

"Hmmm," I said fuzzily. I looked down into my bowl and was disappointed to find it empty. Hopefully I said: "That pleasant surprise you promised—another tankard of scrotch?"

"No, Harold Prodkins. Something you like much better. You ready, I think."

I thought to myself that nothing could be better than another bowl of scrotch. That flea, I now knew, had gone into a convulsion of ecstasy and dived into heaven after only one taste. Almost, I asked Crog to give me scrotch instead of whatever he was planning on.

Then I heard giggling. My pulse raced. I rotated on my stool.

There, just emerged from an adjoining apartment, were three Prunian females—the three who had had the room near ours on board the *Comet's Tail*! Stunned half out of my scrotch daze, I felt my mouth agape. But who could blame them for wanting to be rid of the bug-captained scow?

As though from a long way off I heard Crog say: "Meet three Prunian charmers—Plu, Blu and Flu. True humanoids, if mobile-faced (we all have our faults); loyal to the cause of Strumbermia."

Plu stuck out her ballooning front and giggled. "We meet Harold Prodkins aboard another ship," she said, her tone gurgling.

Blu switched her more-than-ample hips and giggled. "One of us see Harold Prodkins in corridor as he leave ship with Jam brat and Strumbermian." Hers was a drowning tone.

Flu giggled and held her naked tail out at waist level. Playfully she did things with its tip. Things I knew I would once have thought objectionable. "He not know *which* that was!" she gargled. "And she too busy with handsome Strum to invite him in for party!"

I sat frozen. I dared not move.

Crog touched me with his stony forefinger. "Which you want, Harold Prodkins?"

"Which—?" My mind strove to answer the question but balked at understanding it. Crog couldn't mean—no, certainly he couldn't mean that!

"He's cute," said Plu, coiling her tail about my arm. The tail tip drifted, massaged, performed expert indecencies. Nice indecencies.

Blu moved close and rubbed huge conical breasts against me. Round, yet hard; pointed, yet firm— not quite what I had anticipated. "I like," she gurgled.

Flu pushed Blu aside. "My turn—you had Strum before!" Quick as a striking snake she circled my waist with a hairy arm, her tail darted, touched, stroked—not randomly.

Warmth. Heedless. Unashamed. Caring nothing for a world of bag-dresses and pretense. Desire.

The view of a triangular shadow under the lifted tail.

I grabbed the Prunian and took good hold on her, one hand high on that tail.

"In there!" Crog said. His finger pointed through the doorway.

Yet I hesitated. Flu half lifted me, half carried, half dragged. It was only part of me that was unwilling, and not the essential part. Only a part that shied like a frightened stallion at the sight of the waiting pallet. I felt myself reacting as the door slammed.

"I next!" cried Plu from the other side.

"No, me!" said Blu.

"Prunians forget Big Shot Leader!" Crog complained. "Crog got enough for any two Prunians. See?" Several loud squeals set my already heated blood pounding.

I looked into Flu's newborn-baby face. Smoky eyes glowed, flared as from newly banked coals. Her suggestive tail came up, hovered near her skirt, and unsnapped its fastenings.

Clothing fell. Flu stood regarding me in all her primeval naturalness. She stepped from the skirt, removed the blouse. Finally she dropped her single undergarment.

Something in me tried to protest. Better dishonor than death—was that it? I tried to think but couldn't seem to remember. My head swam and my nostrils filled with the musk of a body that was all lust and all promise. What should I do about it? What did I want to do? Was it, could it be—*right?*

My Little Humanoid, Flu thought admiringly, *that was one mighty passion-scream!*

~~~~~~~~ **Chapter 10** ~~~~~~~~

CROG pointed to the huge clinker on the viewing screen. "New Strumbermia Six-O-Five," he said. "Prepare yourself, Harold Prodkins. We land."

"I don't know, Crog," I said from my stool. "Do you really think your Big Shot Commander will accept Earthians as True Humanoids?"

"If you prove," Crog said.

"Can I prove it, Crog? Do I want to?"

Crog made an almost human shrug. "Why you not know, after scrotch and Prunian?"

I looked into his expressionless face. "I'd *like* to know." Why did I feel this way—certain of my facts—yet hesitant? It wasn't as though the scrotch and Prunian could still be affecting me. I'd slept for hours. But something—something—

"You worried about your friends?" Crog asked.

"Friends? You mean Plu, Blu and Flu?"

Crog looked at one of the unstarred Strumbermians and lowered an eyelid. "Mean female Earthian and Jam brat."

"Oh, those. Yes, of course." But it was an overstatement. I was hardly worried about a prude and a worm. What had either ever done for me except make trouble?

"You want go back? Be with them for landing?"

"Doesn't seem worth the effort."

Crog grunted politely. He called my attention to our pilot, who was maneuvering the ship into orbit. I watched the strong Strum hands, reminded of how superior hands were to tentacles or other unnatural appendages.

We slid into the atmosphere. Boiling black sky. Jagged black mountains. Oceans of dirty white hue, like uncured scrotch. Beautiful.

We passed over a large fortress fast to a mountainside. I had the impression of needlelike cannon pointing at us, a rounded dome-roof tapering to a jutting base bearded with packed snow. Many strange crawly things, fit only for stepping on—except that they were, I realized, twenty or thirty feet long. Then we were going down, down, down—dropping into a narrow valley to a perilously constricted space field.

The screen turned darker as we lowered. There was wind or rain or something obscuring it—massed hailstones, maybe. When this did not pass I realized that we had landed.

Crog looked at me obliquely. "You still prisoner. You go ahead to airlock. Worm and female there."

"Yes, Big Shot Leader," I said. Technically he was right, but I certainly didn't *feel* like a prisoner. I trotted down the corridor. I like to see the ship's rats scuttle ahead. I kicked at one who was slow and lame. Damned weakling!

The inner lock was closed, and I waited impatiently for it to open. When I finally got out into the cargo port I saw what looked like an overgrown landcrab crouching at the exit. *IS VEHI-*

CLE! Crog thought. Interesting—he could communicate just as well from a distance, and knew what I was doing though out of sight. I had somehow thought telepathy was a close-range phenomenon. I'd better find out how far thought could travel. . . .

The vehicle wasn't really buglike up close, though I knew it to be the same as the ones I'd seen from above. In fact, it looked like a magnificent piece of machinery. It would be a much more comfortable way of departing the ship than my entry had been. Though why the thought of walking in space should have bothered me I could not say. Spacewalking was *fun*.

I heard feeble footfalls and obnoxious slithering and turned to see Nancy and Qumax.

"Harold!" Nancy cried. For a moment I was afraid she was going to put her flabby arms around me, but she didn't, fortunately. "I was worried I'd never see you again!"

"I'm fine," I said, repressing a spasm of disgust. This pink-cheeked prude imagined that I cared for her! Remembering those glorious moments with Flu, I wondered what even an enlightened Earthian female (let alone Nancy's type!) could possibly do to match them.

Did they torture you, Harold Prodkins? Qumax thought irritatingly.

"No, they didn't, worm," I said. "The Big Shot Leader merely explained things. I feel that he's given me a real education." My skin crawled as I looked at this soft larva, but I realized that it would be wisest to conceal my proper distaste for the time being.

Crog stomped out and motioned us into the vehicle. *I DRIVE!* I went up the steps, which were each a foot too high for me. Nancy scrambled

along, her scrawny thighs showing pinkly through
new tears in her coveralls. I wished she wouldn't
embarrass me by advertising her weakness and
softness. Once her clammy hand brushed against
me and I jerked aside. The worm made a few
half-hearted humping attempts, then waited stupidly until two Strumbermians hoisted him. To
think that I had ever associated with this poor
excuse for a creature!

Inside was a lengthy surface for Qumax to stretch
out on, and padded stools for Nancy and me.
Strumbermians strapped us down. Crog strapped
himself into the driver's stool. He did things with
some knobs.

The ship's outer lock opened and our vehicle
lurched through. It walked on pointed stilts, the
cab elevated a few feet in the air. The steps re-
tracted into the underbody, making the center section partially streamlined. The machine crawled
outside and dropped to a gravite-cushioned landing field.

I turned in my seat and looked out at the curve
of the ship. It was big and seemed to be sphere-
shaped. I saw more Strums clustered about the
base. There were squat buildings and other vehicles much like our own. I marveled at the clean,
functional lines. Nothing ridiculously fancy here!

We moved out beyond the curve of the ship.
Now a high wind buffeted us, and the tractor
lurched and trembled like a drunken daddy-long-
legs, depressing as that image was. What fun!

The melancholy sky was pleasant. I loved that
starless black. High spires like the sere bones of a
weathered corpse rose up on the horizon. Stark,
simple, lovely.

Our machine adjusted its strides to the buffet-
ing. We traveled away from the field. Faster and

faster, jogging along toward the jags. Then up into
the icy peaks! Pleasant drafts of snow leaked inside and speckled us. Huge batlike things flapped
and wheeled overhead, ice splintering off their
wings. Then as we climbed the sleet, oddly, became rain. Great gouts of gluey substance struck
the windshield and adhered until scraped away
with a wiper built like a snowplow. The color was
spectacular.

*BRIGHT RAIN, RED RAIN, COLOR OF FRESH
DRAWN BLOOD RAIN!*

It was Crog, mentally humming his tune of joy
and homecoming. I had not realized he had such
esthetic sensitivities.

Ahead a broken-skull structure clung fast to a
cliffside. It was a huge building, sturdy and handsome—in fact, it was the fortress I had seen during
the descent.

Beside me, Nancy shivered. "Frankenstein's castle," she said, impressed.

I demurred. No Earthly castle could have been
as fine as this.

Crog piloted the vehicle straight up the cliffside.
It crawled through an eye socket and dropped into
a sinus cavity. Enormous guns crowded in on every side, dwarfing those of Lucifernia, so that there
was barely a path between them and the ammuni-
tion conveyors. Hooded Strums watched the sky
and landscape, and I knew that every cannon was
loaded and primed. Very good.

With a new, prancing step the vehicle walked
through toothy portals, bypassed a dark passage
leading downwards (the throat?) and took one of
several maggot-galleries. At its end a large door
raised and we went through a parking area. Crog
braked, the machine settled, and the stairs pushed
down. We unbuckled.

"Harold, don't you think—" Nancy began.

NOT COMMUNICATE, FEMALE! Crog directed her. Good for him!

She silenced. I dismounted from the stool, anxious to get to the Strumbermian higher councils and prove that Earthians were True Humanoids. Soon now!

Nancy was inept with her straps, having difficulty getting loose. I ignored her. Too bad Flu hadn't come along!

Qumax wiggled loose and went to untangle Nancy. We got out and down and walked ahead of Crog. Down halls uncoated with gravite. Up steep stairs unequipped with moving belts or antigravity columns. The worm skidded on the slick of ice that covered some portions, and barely got over the stairs. Crog, naturally, had no trouble; Strums were strong humanoids, who did not dissipate themselves with foolish luxuries.

We stopped after traversing a labyrinth. We were at a room: three bare stone pallets, window overlooking the abyss, no heat, no decorations, a single feeding trough right above an elimination hole. Good accommodations. Crog shoved worm and female inside, but gestured me to accompany him.

"Harold!" Nancy cried as I turned to leave.

NOT COMMUNICATE, PRISONER!

"I'm just going to prove that Earthians are True Humanoids," I said, more for the worm's benefit than hers.

"Harold Prodkins," the brat said, "you must not—"

SILENCE, WORM!

But the pesky Jamborang larva didn't know when to quit. *Harold Prodkins, you must not do this thing!*

Crog raised a finger and pointed at him. Qumax cringed as if struck. He rumpled out of the way. I shoved Nancy clear and went through the doorway. Crog slammed the solid stone door and shoved home the bolt, and we departed.

PREPARE. NOW YOU MEET BIG SHOT COMMANDER PHUG. PROVE SELF TRUE HUMANOID.

We ascended more stairs, then entered a large room with a high dome ceiling. In fact, it was a gravbop court, much larger than any I had seen before. There was a good-sized audience, mainly Strumbermians but including a few sexy Prunians and similar females. No less than thirty Strum leaders squatted around the edge of the wall. One had three stars on his forehead.

Across the court was a diminutive Strum I guessed to be scarcely out of the toddling stage. I thought this youngster cute: a pale, sober ghoul with attractive gimlet eyes.

Three Stars leaned forward and thought at me: *I BIG SHOT COMMANDER PHUG. HAROLD PRODKINS, REPRESENTATIVE OF EARTH, YOU WISH JOIN STRUMBERMIANS? UNITE IN CRUSADE OF TRUE HUMANOIDS?*

I swallowed, suddenly uncertain. Why *wasn't* I certain? "I don't know," I said.

Commander Phug's wine-red eyes bored at Crog. Crog evidently thought something back at him on closed circuit. I could sense, but not positively detect, a mind block.

Crog gripped my shoulder gently, his fingers bending my collarbone only moderately and giving me a slight electric shock. *YOU NEED PROVE SELF TO BIG SHOT COMMANDER, HAROLD PRODKINS. PROVE EARTHIANS TRUE HUMANOIDS.*

"By gravbop?" My mind reeled. If only I did not feel this weakling doubt!

HOW ELSE HUMANOIDS PROVE SELVES? WE CIVILIZED!

Well, that did make sense. But then I became confused again. "I've never—I mean, Earthians don't have gravbop."

There was an ominous murmur and stomping of feet, and I realized that all the Strums were listening in to the dialogue and probably my private thoughts as well, and that I was showing reprehensible, almost buglike uncertainty.

NO MATTER, Crog thought at me, and I could tell he was gruffly embarrassed for me. After all, I was his protégé. *JUST FRIENDLY CIVILIZED CONTEST. NOMINAL. YOU NOT AGAINST CHAMPION—ONLY BEGINNER WHO NEVER BOPPED BEFORE.*

Still, ridiculously, I hesitated. "Can—can I refuse?"

Again the swell of outrage. I was insulting the entire elite class of humanoids, and making a fool out of my sponsor Crog. Very bad form.

REFUSE? THEN YOU NOT TRUE HUMANOID! WE TREAT EARTHIANS AS BUGS AND WORMS!

I already had some notion what that meant. But was I hesitating because I didn't approve of the system, or because I was a coward? Was I really opposed to killing or dying for a good cause?

I made the only possible decision.

"Where's my opponent, Crog?"

Crog indicated the youngster in the far court.

"No, not him, Crog!" I cried. "Not this child!"

"Yes, her," Crog said. "Female name's Ogue. Not matter if she damaged in head by gravbop. Breed just the same. Sooner, even."

I swallowed and tried desperately to think of some way out, and as always my mind tumbled over itself under the pressure and fell flat. I did not really want to—yet it looked to me as though I had no choice. While I was thinking, Crog left and returned with two gravbop poles.

Some stupid holdover from a flabby former life made me say it. "Crog, I'll gravbop, but not with this innocent little girl."

Crog glowered impressively. "You want adult Strumbermian, Mobile-Face? You want Crog? Crog champion!"

Stunned, I watched the young Strum girl hefting poles identical to those I had. Surely I could prevent myself from hurting her if I wished. While if I bopped with Crog, I would get pasted to the wall. Besides, what had this toddler ever done for me?

I took the gravbop poles and hefted them the way the youngster had done. Each pole was about five feet long and tapered from an inch-wide butt to a blunt quarter-inch tip. They were flexible but not flimsy. Such an instrument, if swung sidewise against a body, would hurt; rammed endwise, it would possibly kill. I swung my pair back and forth a few times. The poles balanced naturally in my hands—almost as though they belonged there.

The young female was waiting. I walked up to my side of the net. I raised my poles and the pole tips touched formally. The Strumbermian was the same height as I, but stockier.

Again, something from my softer, less rational Earthian existence made me think to her: *I'll take it easy. I won't hurt you, child.*

I'll crack your foreign skull! she shot back.

Then the small spinning ball was lowered from a box of Strumbermians. I eyed its floating descent and turned my attention to the box containing the tag-lights. They emerged: four. A whistle blew shrilly.

Ogue moved with a speed and dexterity that were dazzling. Crack, crack, crack! the poles cracked. Feint, guard and thrust. Biff, bop, and my cheek stung. Whop! and I was stumbling backwards.

With a head-ringing sense of unreality I watched the batted gravball sail over my side of the net. I moved to block it, but too late. It struck one of my tag-lights, and the globe died.

Furiously I batted the ball back. It zipped over the net, not at all where I wanted it. Lazily, contemptuously, my opponent batted it back, straight for another tag-light.

I intercepted it this time and tried for one of hers. Back and forth, back and forth. Running, leaping, bopping, I sweated. Neither of us could get a clear shot. Even in reduced gravity it was tiring.

I tripped and missed the ball—and there went another of my tag-lights! I bopped back angrily, not even coming close to my opponent's light.

WHOP!

My head wobbled on its hinges. I thought my right ear had been torn off. Feebly I batted the ball that had just struck me.

WHOP!

The ball returned and struck me again. I had forgotten that all was fair in gravbop. I had been geared to intercept shots at my tag-lights, and had not guarded my head! I was down on my knees now, blood staining my cheek. Dizzily I saw my opponent run close to the net and reach a pole across. Horrified, I realized that she intended to brain me—and with that leverage, she could do it!

Driven by a desperation I would not have believed, I blocked with a pole. But with a flick of her wrist, Ogue altered her swing and struck the floating gravball.

BOP!

That was the third of my tag-lights. But in striking the ball my adversary left an opening, and she was in range. I swung my raised pole.

CRUNCH!

Ogue collapsed against the net, bleeding from the ear. Emotionlessly, I raised the pole and brought it down hard on her forehead.

She fell all the way to the floor. She had been careless, and now was paying the consequence. I struggled to my feet and made for the gravball.

Bop, and I missed the tag-light I had aimed for. I retrieved the ball with a pole-flip and tried again. Again I missed. Have to lead, I thought—as in wing-shooting or Solar Pool.

I shot and missed four times in a row. Each time the ball either bounced back to my side, or slowly drifted within range of my cue. The gravite seemed to be tilted, in effect, making it roll in mid-air toward the net. Though why the players weren't affected. . . .

On the sixth try I succeeded in hitting a tag-light. I felt a surge of self-confidence. I was finally getting the hang of it.

One down and three to go—for me. But now Ogue was dragging herself upright. I bopped her down again and went about my business.

Four more shots got me another of her tag-lights. Three more got the third. One more shot . . . and I connected with the last of Ogue's lights.

A mental cheer went up. I felt triumph. I was an expert gravbopper and a big hairy-chested True Humanoid! I looked at Ogue and saw how well I had downed her. She might grow up to breed, but that was about all.

But I had not really put this on the proper footing yet. The importance of Earth had been underrated. She should not have to join the Humanoid movement on the Strumbermians' terms; she should negotiate from a position of power.

Crog had acted all along as if I were a weakling, barely able to establish myself on the gravbop court. And Phug had gone along with that. Imagine—pitting me against a female child! Me, an expert Solar Pool player, and now a pretty good gravbopper as well! Why, with a little more practice I could be as good as any of them.

Hell, I was that good right now.

Big Shot Leader Crog! I challenged boldly.

YES MOBILE FACE?

You want a deciding contest—you and me?

That put him on notice! *WHAT STAKES, MOBILE FACE?*

"You defeat me in full gravbop contest and I'll pledge Earth to support the crusade. I defeat you"—let's see, I wanted this to hurt—"and you'll release all prisoners from the Comet's Tail and provide passage to a neutral world where we can contact Jamborango, and"—now what would really tie it up?—"and extend apologies to all concerned and make reparations to the worms and bugs for the inconvenience."

Crog gaped at me.

"Deal, Stoneface?"

DEAL! DEAL! DEAL! commanded the audience. *IS CONTEST! IS CONTEST!* Boy, were they mad!

Three-star Phug raised a large hand. *TOMORROW WE HOLD MATCH—HAROLD PRODKINS VERSUS BIG SHOT LEADER CROG IN STAKED CONTEST. EIGHT TAG-LIGHTS, OTHER PRISONERS WITNESS.*

Crog smiled. Mentally.

Looking at his horrible supertoothed countenance I had an abrupt letdown. Suddenly I didn't feel like a True Humanoid at all. I felt like the conned sucker who wakes to find himself the Judas goat.

~~~~~~~ Chapter 11 ~~~~~~~

Qumax rumpled agitatedly across the floor of our new quarters. His worm-head turned and his dark eyes flashed. *"You are a fool, Harold Prodkins!"* he said and thought.

"Am I, Qumax?" I mumbled from my pallet. He was probably right, but I didn't like to have a mere larva point it out. I watched the back of Nancy's blonde head as she stood staring out at a sickish orange sunrise. I hadn't told her about yesterday. It had seemed best not to rush it.

"Yes! It's an old Strumbermian trick. First they raise their victim's confidence—then they get the fool to challenge. Believe me, Harold Prodkins, an Earthian hasn't a chance against a Strumbermian gravbop champion."

"Are you certain?"

"Certain."

"Do you take me for a coward? Do you think Earth would stand a better chance against the Strumbermians than I will in gravbop? Do you prefer the chance in war?"

134

"There is NO chance for you in gravbop. You made a deal with the Strumbermians; it will be they who keep it for you. You've just pledged your planet to their crusade!"

Somehow that prospect seemed much worse than it had a day ago. At the time it had not seemed unreasonable that Earth be allied to Strumbermia, suppressing the vermin of the galaxy. Now I wondered why I had not considered the intellectual factors, which would have thrown the balance the other way. "What makes you think I can't at least manage to get myself killed?"

"Harold!" Nancy interjected.

"That would lose the match," Qumax said relentlessly. "Haven't you learned anything yet? Do you think getting your brains knocked out will change anything? Lots of people get killed in gravbop. Strumbermians play to WIN!"

"So do I!" I said. "And I'm going to—someway."

Nancy turned from the window and its unearthly view. "I know you gravbopped last night," she said. "Qumax told me while it was happening."

So not all my dizziness had been from blows to the head! The worm had been snooping, maybe interfering!

"It's not just your lack of skill—" the brat said insultingly.

"What, then?"

"The nature of the Strumbermians. Adults can release energy from their fingers—electrical energy."

I peered at the overgrown cabbage worm. No, he wasn't hoaxing me. Suddenly I understood why the Strums pointed fingers so frequently, and why I had felt a shock when touched by one. Like electric eels, they generated current to make an effective close-range weapon.

"Crog can use this energy in gravbop?" But I

knew even as I asked. Anything went in gravbop, so long at it was inherent in the player and situation. Devians had used their reach, Strumbermians could use their electricity. What could a man use?

"The range is quite short, Harold Prodkins. About three of the Strum's body-lengths. But if you come closer—"

"Hm. That big court is about a hundred feet—fifty per side. That gives me some maneuvering room. . . ."

"More like eighty feet, forty per side. Over half of which is open to Crog's charge. If you stay in the back fifteen feet, you may be able to stay alive, if you duck the beanballs. Provided Crog wants you alive."

"No, it won't be easy," I admitted. I looked at the composition soles and heels of my shoes and wondered if these would be any help as insulators. Possibly, and then again, possibly not. I couldn't be certain whether this really was electricity, despite what Qumax said. It might be something else that followed different rules.

"Why did you do it, Harold?" Nancy asked me softly.

I looked at her and wondered how I could ever have imagined her to be attractive. Small bulges in front, pale head of hair, moderate hips, disgustingly mature face. And no tail!

But attractive or not, she did deserve some explanation. She was, after all, still technically my assistant, and she did mean well. So I set out to clarify my motives—

And found that I could not come across with anything that sounded good in words or specific thoughts. Odd.

*   *   *

Three hours into cold daylight we were taken to the court. Fifteen minutes later I was facing Crog across the gravbop net, armed with the twin poles. I peered past his bulky, blocky frame as I waited for the whistle. Nancy perched on a stool beside Big Shot Commander Phug, her head averted. Qumax lay nearby, eyes bright and staring at me. They expected me to lose, I knew. It was for that they had been brought here.

Crog and I touched poles. *We who are about to die salute you*, I thought at the audience, and wondered why I bothered. First whistle blew and the small ball lowered. Eight tag-lights flashed on either side.

The fighting whistle sounded. Crog swung his poles. I ducked and dropped flat, rolling back out of reach. I figured he wouldn't use his finger-charge right away; he'd wait until he needed it. But all the same, I was going to get out of range and stay out.

I heard the bop of cue striking ball.

Clasping only one of my poles, I rolled over and over across the gravcourt. A pole banged down behind me, scraping skin off my left shoulder; Crog had a long reach. Ahead, the gravball put out one of my tag-lights.

I got my pole up and stopped the ball. I could not afford to let it drift to the center. I rose to my feet, moved behind the ball and lifted my pole in both hands. Gently I tapped the spinning sphere until it floated just at shoulder height. I stepped back, raised the pole, and sighted down it as though it were a Solar Pool cue.

This was just like Solar Pool, in fact, I told myself. The nearest tag-light was the Venus sphere, the ball—the cueball. I had played such a game many times; in fact, I had once contemplated en-

tering a world tournament, back on Earth, for the
Solar Pool championships. But Freddy had squelched
that. It wasn't that he had lacked confidence in my
ability (though he did); it was that it would have
looked trivial on his political record. A pool-playing
cousin.

I drew back the pole and aimed the ball at the
light. I took a deep breath and expelled half. Careful now. Careful. I had done this easily yesterday.
This cue was straight and true, just a trifle heavy.

The Venus sphere floated and bobbed in a manner
no Venus sphere should ever do. Yet I had com-
pensated automatically as I put out Ogue's final
light. There, now, the sphere's motion was carrying it toward me. It was a setup for a Solar Pool
champ. Or a hopeful champ. Shoot, I told myself,
and my practiced muscles reacted accordingly.

The gravball went like a meteor. Pow! and Crog's
tag-light disappeared.

That broke the ice. I knew I could score, now,
and it wouldn't take me so much concentration
again. I had to operate from far back in the court,
but I had the game in hand.

Crog made his round-mouthed gesture. It was
about all that he was capable of in the way of
facial expression. He must have thought I would
miss from this range. Or be so frightened of him
that I would not be able to shoot at all.

Quickly he fielded the ball and bopped it back at
a tag-light. Toward my left, and I a right-hander.

Now I wished I had both poles, but I transferred
the single one to my left hand and managed clum-
sily to stop this missile. The important thing was
to keep it on my own side and in my own back-
court, except when shooting.

I bopped it against the wall, stopped it again
with the pole, and started lining things up.

Terrible screams and mind-blasts of indignation came from the audience. I was taking plenty of time, letting myself recover fully from the brief spate of exertion. Time-taking and resting were not routine, it seemed. Too bad for them; I was not going to mess up my game by rushing it.

PLAY GRAVBOP! Crog thought at me.

"Patience, frozen-face," I said. "By and by I'll play a game that will knock your wooden block off."

I was rewarded by a mental wash of fury. He was mad now—really mad, not play-acting mad like yesterday. Good.

Three tag-lights floated just right. I designated them Mercury, Jupiter and Earth, and tried for a triple-slam.

And made it! Great slippery moonbeams, was I hot!

POW!

I ducked just enough to avoid Crog's bean ball. The hairs of my head vibrated with the nearness of its passing. I was playing a dangerous game, and not just gravbop, for he was mighty fast and accurate with that ball. But I was on to his tricks and strategy now.

"You ain't seen nothing yet, Frog—I mean Crog," I said as I batted the ball against the backstop a couple of times in order to bring it down to manageable velocity. So long as he stayed mad, he'd fire at me instead of the lights, and that was what I wanted. "You scrotch-sodden, bugfaced, wormlike excuse for a humanoid."

The power of his mental retort made me wince, but I braced myself and aimed carefully. "Try to bop *my* skull, will you?" I said. "Why, you wouldn't know a Prunian from a naked ant-queen, lover boy."

Hell itself could not be more diabolic than the vision he blasted at my mind. I waited for my synapses to cool, and fired.

Two more tag-lights! Six to one in my favor. These Strumbermians had become so enamored of the head-splitting propensities of the game that they had forgotten the advantage of sheer skill.

I sensed Nancy and Qumax cheering me. Lot I cared for that now. They had predicted I'd lose. I didn't need them.

Crog missed a swipe and tried another. He seemed remarkably clumsy; how had he ever risen to the championship? Must be breaking down under the sheer strain of losing, the big sissy. The gravball flew, but wobbly. It was an even worse serve than my own first faltering attempts.

The ball hit the wall on my side, bounced against the net, rebounded, slowed, stopped. It floated four feet above the floor, ten feet in front of me. I stepped toward it, keeping a wary eye on my opponent. I did not want to get within reach of his pole!

Stop, Harold Prodkins!

I froze, caught with one foot not quite down. That was Qumax's itchy message! Overcautious worm! I looked at Crog and judged him to be just over twenty feet away. I could afford one more step, then a lunge for the ball. Otherwise, Crog would recover the initiative, and I could not count on him to give it back. I took the step.

At that moment a flare went off. Crog's entire body was outlined in a bright purple nimbus. A bolt of energy struck me broadside. I could have sworn sparks radiated from my hair. I had twin hotfoots: the soles of my shoes were melting.

A second passed in agony. Two seconds. Two hours? Two eternities. I stood frozen/burning, immobilized. I thought the fillings in my teeth were roasting, my eyeballs frying. Forever times infinity, it continued.

Then, as abruptly as it had begun, the nimbus ceased. Crog seemed smaller, depleted. But he moved up to the net.

I stumbled backwards. Crog reached over the net, trying to hook the gravball. I collapsed flat on the court, seeking to die there and sift down through the cracks into peace. How I could still be conscious I didn't know. Perhaps there was something to the notion that you could become partially immune to the effects of low-voltage shocks. Or maybe my composition soles *had* alleviated the effect.

Get up, Harold! Get up!

That was Nancy's thought. I would have hated any female for it.

Hurry, Harold!

When had she mastered mindtalk? I struggled to my feet, wishing I could belt her one.

Crog retrieved the ball. He bopped it—hard. His prior ineptitude had been a ruse. To lure me within range of—this.

Dully I watched it zip by my nose and knock off two of my tag-lights. So the ape *could* make sophisticated shots when he tried! I raised my pole as the ball bounced from the wall and headed for my face. Sphere collided with pole and bounced near net. Crog retrieved.

YOU AIN'T SEEN NOTHIN' YET, MOBILE-FACE!

So now Crog was bragging, hamming it up.

BIFF!

Incredulously I watched the ball pick off one, two, three of my tag-lights, and barely miss a fourth! Had Crog only been toying with me all along? The ball rebounded from the wall and drifted toward the net.

Harold, stop that ball! Nancy's thought came. *Stop it this instant!*

But Crog already had it. He bopped it without even seeming to aim, but I knew that shot would finish the game. The ball passed through my seventh light, ricocheted off the back wall, and sped unerringly for my eighth.

I threw myself desperately in front of my last bastion.

I stopped the ball. Right in the belly.

I fell down with a terrible whoof of expelled air, but even as I toppled my left hand clasped the ball to my gut.

Shoot, Harold! You've got to shoot!

Pesty female! Give me time and I'd fix her!

Lights whirled—few of them tag-lights. My stomach was agony, and I feared that a splinter of bone was grinding into one lung.

I had the cue-ball. I focused on the nearest light, lining up ball and pole, calculating, aiming, for I would not get another shot. I tensed—

No!

My cue jerked, ruining my shot. The ball skidded a few feet sideways. That had been Qumax's itch!

"Which side are you on, worm-brat?" I demanded.

That was your own tag-light!

I snapped alert. He was right!

I corralled the ball again—fortunately it had drifted away from Crog—and set up properly. There were two lights over on his side. Neptune sphere and Pluto sphere, I designated them. I put the ball out in the air ahead of me, lifted my cue, and aimed it from where I sat.

There were crowd noises. Part of the audience did not like my taking so much time. *Bug you!* I thought at them.

Neptune sphere occluded Pluto sphere. *Shoot!* I told myself. *SHOOT!*

I froze. Had that been *my* thought? Why wasn't Crog lambasting me?

My head cleared a little more. That last suggestion had been Crog's, not mine. He was poised, ready to intercept the ball, then bat it back at my own light before I could get up again. Even if I got one of his, I would lose.

I stood up, walked around the ball once, made a feint at the occluded lights, twisted—and let fly with a surprise shot directly at Crog's head, putting all my power into it.

He ducked reflexively, O-mouthed. The ball caromed off the back wall. I set up as it returned to me and swung without waiting for it to stop: a baseball hit.

The gravball cleared the net. A trifle off course. But only a trifle. Crog, seeing what I had done, lurched to his feet and dived for it . . . too late.

B-Bop! No more Neptune sphere.

Pause.

BOP-P! No more Pluto sphere.

Victory.

I had just made my greatest shot ever—and knew I would never duplicate it.

Crowd noises. Crowd thoughts. Some cheered me for winning. Others thought my slow tactics should disqualify me.

Nancy and Qumax left the side of Commander Phug and came out on the floor. Nancy took my arm before I sat down from sheer relief and letdown. Suddenly all my pains returned in full force. I groaned and held my stomach where the ball had punched. I didn't mind Nancy's touch at all, now.

Crog faced his superior. A concession speech?

*MOBILE-FACED CREATURE HAS NOT WON.
GRAVBOP ALWAYS PLAYED FAST. EARTHIAN
TOO SLOW. HE CHEATED!*

Oh, come now! I thought privately. How could I
be accused of cheating when there *were* no fouls in
gravbop? If braining your opponent was fair, so
was teasing him, and so was taking proper time
for shots.

Phug stroked his chin, and I knew he was going
to reprimand his subordinate for his poor sportsmanship.

*YOU RIGHT, CROG. EARTHIAN'S STRATEGY
TRICKY LIKE BUG. UNWORTHY OF HUMANOID.*

What?

"No!" Nancy cried. "Harold won fairly, according to your rules, Strumbermian Big Shot Commander!"

SILENCE, FEMALE EARTHIAN!

I picked up a swell of agreement from the crowd.
Agreement with Phug, not Nancy. I saw the lay of
it now.

"Don't interfere, Nancy," I said. *They're just trying
to pretend they didn't lose. Strumbermians can't face
facts.*

Phug pondered. I knew my mental crack had
scored. If he declared Crog victor now, everyone
present would know he had backed off from an
accusation of fixing the fight.

Phug stroked his granite chin again. *WE PLAY
MORE GRAVBOP. THIS TIME FAST. CROG, EARTH-
IAN—THREE MORE TAG-LIGHTS.*

"He won't do it," Nancy said, and I was too
weak to protest. I had to admit, though, that she
looked and sounded much better than she had half
an hour ago. It was as though all the striving and
banging had resettled my synapses. "Commander
Phug, Harold Prodkins refuses to gravbop again."

Phug rose from his stool. *EARTHIAN WISH TO BE SAME AS BUGS AND WORMS? NOT TRUE HUMANOID? BE OUR ENEMY?*

"Yes!" Nancy cried.

Phug shook his head ponderously. *FOOLS! LEADER CROG, RETURN PRISONERS TO CELL. TREAT BAD—THEY NOT TRUE HUMANOIDS!*

Crog looked sadistically delighted. I looked at Nancy as the giant tore open the net and approached with leveled finger. "Now you've done it!" I said.

"You aren't sorry, are you, Harold?"

"I—" *Was* I? To gravbop on Phug's terms would be to lose. Earth would become part of the crusade because of the terms I'd made. Did I really want that? To lose to Crog and see my home world become another Strumbermia? Earth—what would it be, New Strumbermia Six-O-Six? Confusion made my head whirl.

Crog towered over us, grimacing toothily.

Then:

STRUMBERMIANS AND EARTHIANS! STRUMBERMIANS AND EARTHIANS AND JAMBORANGO INFANT! an amplified thought intruded. *THIS IS THE GALACTIC POLICE! THIS IS THE GALACTIC POLICE!*

My right hand clutched Nancy's left. There were startled and dismayed thoughts. Then no one in the room was communicating.

The entire overhead dome became transparent. In the beautiful—well, impressive—black sky were hundreds, possibly thousands, of needle-shaped starcraft.

A wailing thought went up from Phug, chilling because so un-Strumbermian: *DEFEAT, DEFEAT, DEFEAT!*

"We not even have combat," Crog said, a huge

tear running down his pallid cheek, and I almost felt sorry for him. "Not even know. Bugs come while we absorbed with contest. We trapped."

SPOKESMAN FOR STRUMBERMIANS, the police thought demanded. *TO AVOID IMMEDIATE ANNIHILATION YOU MUST SURRENDER UNCONDITIONALLY. NOW.*

Phug thought-quavered his craven capitulation. I was amazed at how readily these bold pirates caved in when they lost the advantage. True Humanoids, indeed!

SPOKESMAN FOR EARTHIANS?

I hesitated. "Hurry!" Qumax said. "They have quivery trigger-tendrils."

Taking a good grip on my mixed emotions, I thought loudly: *I Harold Prodkins, Minister etc. of Earth, do hereby officially and unconditionally surrender all inhabitants of the planet Earth on New Strumbermia Six-O-Five to the lawfully constituted authority of the Galactic Police.*

SPOKESMAN FOR—

"Me too!" Qumax cried.

~~~~~~~~~ **Chapter 12** ~~~~~~~~~

A<small>T</small> the directive of some distant Galactic Police officer, Nancy, Qumax and I returned to the landing field. Crog, expressing no resentment whatever, drove us in the landcrab.

Watching the dark alien landscape jerk by, and the perpetual blast of sleet and nauseous atmospheric mucous, I wondered what I had seen in this planet before. I hoped Jamborango would be better, or at least warmer. Then I wondered if we'd really be going to Jamborango, and if it were really Jams who had captured new Strumbermia Six-O-Five. Or Imbibels, or whatever. I thought a few terse questions at Qumax.

"Harold Prodkins," he replied, "there is no other force in the galaxy powerful enough to take this planet."

"You bet," Crog mumbled.

"*Did* they take it? Seems to me that with the Strumbermians adept at mind communications— well, why wasn't there a warning?"

"Because the police did not allow one."

"But—"

"It would take you many years to understand, Harold Prodkins," the brat said smugly. "They have ways. They dampen out thoughts and deactivate weapons. When they make themselves known with a surrender demand, the wise criminal knows he is already defeated.'"

"And the police are Jams?"

"The police are Inner-Galactics. The one who actually communicated with us happened to be a Jamborang."

"So we'll be taken to Jamborango?"

"Of course!"

"But I still don't see how they found this hideout!"

"I can explain, Harold Prodkins. You remember the cruiser that shot at the raider? And intentionally missed?"

"I remember them missing. . . ."

"And that heroic fight I had in the control room?"

"I remember them beating you," I said. As he deserved, I thought privately.

"The Strums could have found out from my mind, but they are the most arrogant creatures this side of Earth. They thought me too young to have any information of value to them."

I shrugged. Who would blame them for that? "What could they have learned from your mind?"

"The communications equipment had a pattern-disguiser. During ship-to-ship communications it scrambles the out-going electrical patterns in such a way that they cannot be followed. Everything has its characteristic pattern, from the tip of my tail or your forefinger to the most powerful transgalactic transmitter. Such patterns are left in residue form wherever a thing had been in space. These residues, shadows, traces can be detected by sensitive equipment and followed to their source. The process—"

"Spare me the physics, Qumax. I never did understand that slop."

"You asked me how the police found this planet."

I saw that he was determined to have his lecture session. "Keep it short," I said.

"Now at one time a pattern-disguiser had to be off for an appreciable length of time before the police could record and analyze the pattern it disguised. But there have been recent advances that the outlying species have not found out about—notably the Strumbermians. So when, in the course of my supposed frenzy, I flicked off the disguiser for a fraction of a second—"

The vehicle swerved. WHY, YOU—YOU *WORM!* Crog thought, almost mentally speechless with fury. Then he remembered his place and shut up.

"Qumax, you saved all our lives!" Nancy said.

The oversized larva didn't answer. Two large tears formed in his eyes. I noted the drooping antenna. I didn't get it.

"Aren't you glad to be going home?" Nancy asked.

Qumax looped tentacles around both our shoulders. He made his irritating screech-crying noise.

Nancy held her ears. "It shouldn't be too bad, Qumax," she said, trying to comfort him. The crybaby. "Your Swarm Tyrant will welcome you—I'm sure he will. He may punish you a little for playing hooky, but surely it won't be *that* bad."

"It isn't—screech—*my* punishment I'm concerned about."

We both waited until he got his tears under control. "Whose, then?" I asked.

"Yours."

I wasn't sure whether to laugh. "My—punishment?"

"Scre-e-e-e-ch," Qumax, or sounds to that effect.

I waited again. When he settled down I asked: "What am I guilty of? My mission on behalf of Earth undertaken without what some arrogant Jam thinks is adequate reason?"

"No, Harold Prodkins."

"Incurring too much in passenger fares, at Jam expense? Getting captured by Strums? Walking on the grass? Make sense, worm!"

"More serious. Much more serious. You are in deep trouble for making a deal with the Strumbermians. For wagering with them in gravbop."

"But I WON, Qumax. Besides, I had no choice."

"You thought you had no choice. You are a representative of your world, and yet you let fear dominate your reasoning. You agreed to gravbop and in fact suggested it as a way out. Does that seem like worthy thinking?"

"Since I was prepared to win, I think it very worthy!"

"There's the landing field," Nancy said.

"I *see* the landing field, Qumax, are you accusing me of cowardice, you bug-eyed worm?"

"There's one of the police craft," Qumax said.

Qumax, you answer me!

"It will be you who will have to answer, Harold Prodkins—and not to me. If you're sure of your answers, perhaps you can convince yourself and maybe then you can convince ... but leave me alone."

"I'll leave you alone, worm!" I was furious, yet as soon as I had expressed myself I felt ashamed for it. I decided to say something more civilized. "This planet—it's only one of the Strumbermians', isn't it?"

"Only one, and that a minor one. Only a few thousand inhabitants."

"Must be a lot of Strumbermians in the galaxy."

"A very lot. And they will do well enough as long as they can trick your kind into joining them."

"They haven't tricked mine yet!"

"Yes, they have. Fortunately, my action brought the police in time to save you from your folly."

"Qumax, you brat—" But then Crog stopped the vehicle next to the needle-shaped police craft. The cab lowered; the steps came out and down. Nancy, Qumax and I got out. Qumax almost fell. He was still weak from the beating he had received. This time I did, in spite of myself, feel sorry for him, and I helped him down.

The cab elevated. The machine walked off at a good wind-bucking speed. *So long, Crog, you smileless excuse for a humanoid!* I fired at him.

Farewell, Mobile-Face, Sucker!

We entered the empty police ship. We humans sat on small seats while Qumax stretched himself on a longer one. He groaned from the bruises he still had.

The lock shut. A light-colored gas infiltrated the compartment, making my head swim.

"Breathe deeply," Qumax advised. "When we wake up we'll be on Jamborango. And we'll be much recovered, physically and mentally and emotionally."

I doubt it, I thought, and realized that I was unreasonably scared.

"Have no fear, Harold Prodkins. You will not be allowed to die until you have stood trial—and even then, maybe not."

I saw that Nancy's eyes were glazed. It occurred to me that there was something unpleasantly suggestive about the way Qumax had phrased that. I wanted to think, but—

I felt the ship lurch under me. I drew a deep

breath, not able to help myself. I let it out, seemingly only seconds later, and as I looked out the port I realized that the worm had known what he was talking about.

The streets looked like silver and the creatures using them were of every shape and color imaginable. Certainly this was not Strumbermia Six-O-Five.

Qumax was already opening the exit-port, Nancy beside him. The worm's motions were vigorous, and he had no bruises or cuts; Nancy's uniform was whole again. And I felt much better myself. As though it were the flick of a trebvee scene shift, our situation had changed. Instead of ending a grueling adventure, we were beginning one.

Well, such was Inner-Galactic technology. I joined them at the door.

The scene was a view from inside a kaleidoscope, and my senses reeled at even beginning to grasp it. I saw that our ship had landed in a cleared area somewhere in the heart of a great city, and I saw that there were streets going by on all sides, and they were stretched out overhead in loops and spirals and arches. I saw fantastically gossamer-winged creatures hovering everywhere, hardly needing the streets, and I marveled at their beauty. These could not be native Jams, for they were unlike Qumax.

"There's Nitti, our old Earth host," said Qumax.

I followed the indication of his tentacles and spotted Warden Nitti. He stood on a podium not far out from our ship. He was, I swear, a thousand feet tall!

"It's a projection of some kind," Nancy said. "Something like our solidifilms—isn't it, Qumax?"

"Closer to trebvee," Qumax said. "It is being

broadcast—to civilized cities throughout the galaxy."

"Then he's not here." Momentarily I felt relief that I did not have the opportunity to destroy the traitor. "Or is he on this world?"

"He's here in this city. This is the Jamborango capital."

I stared at the towering projection. Nitti and his jowly face rotated toward us. He was dressed in an exact duplicate of his dress uniform, complete with cummerbund and Jupegas gun. He looked, I was forced to admit, just about the way a successful prison warden should.

"What's the purpose of this?" I asked. "Don't tell me they're honoring this slob as a hero!"

"The purpose will soon be apparent," Qumax said in that brattish way of his. And then he thought: *I'm sorry, Harold Prodkins; I know how painful this will be for you.*

"Painful! What do you—"

An amplified thought intruded. It seemed to press in from everywhere. *GALACTIC CITIZENS—YOUR ATTENTION!*

Instantly a change came over the street. Traffic stopped moving. Flying creatures folded their wings and settled gently and unobtrusively down among the pedestrians. There was no noise, no vocal or mental communication of any kind from the crowds. A city, a world, and perhaps tens of thousands, hundreds of millions of worlds—waited.

PEOPLES OF WORLDS RICH IN TECHNOLOGY AND COMMERCE. IT IS FITTING THAT WE HONOR ACTS OF HEROISM. WARDEN NITTI, REHABILITATION OFFICIAL OF A DISTANT PRIMITIVE PLANET NAMED EARTH, BELIEVES HIMSELF TO BE THE SYMBOL OF COURAGE AND DEVOTION TO DUTY, IN THE CYNOSURE OF

HIS PLANET'S INHABITANTS. WHEN THE CARGO SHIP, COMET'S TAIL, WAS RECENTLY ATTACKED AND PLUNDERED BY STRUMBERMIANS, HE PERFORMED A FEAT THAT MUST BE UNDERSTOOD WITHIN THE FRAMEWORK OF HIS PSYCHOLOGY. BECAUSE NO ONE ELSE APPEARED TO BE WILLING TO DEAL REALISTICALLY WITH THE STRUMBERMIAN RAIDERS, BY THIS MAN'S DEFINITIONS, HE FORCED HIMSELF TO PORTRAY THE TRAITOR WHILE BELIEVING HIS ACT TO BE THE SENSIBLE AND HEROIC ONE. HE OFFERED HIS TRAVELING COMPANIONS, NANCY DILSMORE OF EARTH AND QUMAX OF JAMBORANGO, IN EXCHANGE FOR HIS OWN FREEDOM AND THE LIVES OF OTHERS. HE DID NOT KNOW THAT THIS MIGHT WELL COST THE SECURITY OF HIS HOME PLANET. HE FELT HIS ACT WOULD PRESERVE A GREATER PROPORTION OF THE SHIP'S COMPLEMENT THAN WOULD OTHERWISE BE POSSIBLE. SUBSEQUENT ANALYSIS SUGGESTS HE WAS CORRECT IN THIS SINGLE CASE. THE STRUMBERMIANS WERE MORE INTERESTED IN CONVERTS THAN IN PLUNDER.

There was a pause in the amplified thought. The projection of Warden Nitti bowed its head slightly as though acknowledging.

WE WHO HAVE THE ADVANTAGE OF ADULTHOOD IN A HIGHLY EVOLVED SOCIETY REALIZE THAT SUCH THINKING VIOLATES THE CODES OF INTERSPECIES MORALITY. NO NEGOTIATIONS SHOULD HAVE BEEN ATTEMPTED WITH THE COMPLETELY AMORAL STRUMBERMIANS. BUT IN HIS OWN MIND, AND BY THE DICTATES OF HIS OWN CULTURE, THERE WAS HEROISM IN WARDEN NITTI'S ACTION. THUS

*WE HAVE HONORED HIS INTENT WHILE DIS-
AVOWING HIS METHOD.*

Again the thought broke off. The lofty image of
Warden Nitti seemed to take on new solidity. Behind his head appeared a huge black circle.

*ONE THOUGHT HAD BEEN PROMINENT IN
WARDEN NITTI'S MIND SINCE HIS RESCUE AND
THE START OF HIS INSTRUCTION. HE WISHES,
ABOVE ALL ELSE, TO BE FORGIVEN BY THOSE
HE HAS WRONGED. THE THREE INDIVIDUALS
WHO WERE HELD CAPTIVE ON NEW STRUM-
BERMIA SIX-O-FIVE NOW HAVE THE OPPOR-
TUNITY TO FORGIVE, OR TO REFUSE TO FOR-
GIVE, THIS GUILT-BOWED FIGURE.*

A gossamer-winged being turned its fine-featured
face our way. With stately stride and flutter it
advanced to our open airlock. In tentacles, very
similar to Qumax's, it carried a fragile-seeming
pink crystal. It halted before us—tall, phenomenally beautiful. It held out the crystal.

Qumax knew what to do. He took the crystal and
held it in his own tentacles.

From the crystal there came a thought. Nitti's.
Will you forgive me, Qumax?

I forgive you, Qumax thought. As naturally as
though he had been doing this every day, he turned
and handed the crystal to Nancy.

Will you forgive me, Nancy Dilsmore?

Nancy hesitated. Her fair brow wrinkled. She
raised her eyes to the winged alien and then looked
beyond it to the gigantic, now perfectly immobile
image. She frowned.

Mr. Nitti, she thought, *I understand why you did
what you did, even though I cannot approve of it. I
do not know what possible benefit it can be to you—
but yes, because I understand, I forgive you.*

Nancy handed me the crystal. It was warm and

as delicate in shape as a single huge snowflake. I stared down into the intricate three-dimensional design—and down inside myself.

And you, Harold Prodkins? Do you also forgive?

In an alien's eye! Filled with righteous indignation, I let him have some of my mind:

Nitti, you are a contemptible excuse for an Earthian. Nothing that I could possibly think now would be adequate to fully express my disgust for you. You are everything a human being should not be, plus a few things that nothing should be. You have a hell of a nerve to beg my forgiveness now—I, whom you betrayed along with Qumax and Nancy. Why didn't you think about forgiveness then, when you weighed our lives against—

And right there I stopped. Nitti had gambled two or three lives in the hope that many more would be saved. I had gambled lives also—the same ones. Viewed this way, wasn't my "crime" as contemptible as his? Couldn't he claim just as logically that he had, indeed, acted heroically?

Please go on, Nitti thought, and I was amazed by the servile aspect of it. *I must know whether you can forgive me.*

I raised my eyes to the distant image. I felt that I should be enjoying the traitor's agony, that I was entitled to some self-righteousness. But somehow— well, in the long run, what could I do? What could *any* imperfect Earthian do? In the end, we have to forgive the Warden Nittis in order to be free of them.

Nitti, I got out in mental chunks, *I know that you are contemptible, but I also know that I—that . . . Oh, let me forgive you and let it go at that.*

In my hands the crystal shimmered and fell apart and dissolved into vapor and was gone. On the face of Nitti's image a faint smile formed. *You have made me happy*, came the thought from the dissipating mist. *I thank each of you . . . whom I have wronged . . . for forgiving me. Now if you will watch the projection. . . .*

We watched. For a moment, nothing. Then the black circle haloing the image seemed to catch fire. A bright green flame enveloped the imaged head, providing it a striking glory. Then the flame was all.

Taut muscles relaxed. Slowly, emptily, the headless body toppled. As it fell it became less distinct. Slower, slower, fainter, fainter—drifting and gaseous, like the remnant of the crystal. Just before it would have struck our ship it vanished. I was relieved, for though I knew it to be only an optical effect, I did not want to be engulfed by the corpse of Warden Nitti.

I had had no idea this was going to happen. Suicide! The guy must really have been serious!

PEOPLE OF THE GALAXY, YOU HAVE JUST WITNESSED THE MERCY-KILLING OF WARDEN NITTI, AN EARTHIAN. IN ACCORDANCE WITH INNER-GALACTIC CUSTOM AND ETHICAL PRINCIPLE, THE DECEASED WAS NOT SUBJECTED TO EXTERNAL PUNISHMENT BUT WAS MADE AWARE OF THE FLAWS IN HIS THINKING AND THE FULL IMPLICATIONS OF HIS BEHAVIOR. HE WAS THEN REQUIRED BY THE DICTATES OF HIS NEWLY AWAKENED CONSCIENCE TO OBTAIN FORGIVENESS FROM HIS CHIEF VICTIMS. HAD WARDEN NITTI BEEN UNSUCCESSFUL IN OBTAINING SUCH FORGIVENESS HE WOULD HAVE BEEN REQUIRED BY THAT SAME CONSCIENCE TO LIVE WITH HIS GUILT AND KEEP TRYING FOR FORGIVENESS FOR AS LONG AS GALACTIC SCIENCE COULD SUSTAIN HIS LIFE. HIS VICTIMS HAVE BEEN MERCIFUL

*AND HAVE GRANTED HIM THE GIFT OF EU-
THANASIA. JUSTICE HAS BEEN DONE.*

The thought ceased. Music, part sound, part
thought, part direct emotion, played. It was the
funeral march for Warden Nitti. The theme swelled
to an almost unbearable intensity, then faded.

The gloom of death descended.

I stood there, reliving that episode in the perspective of its termination. I had supposed it to be
some commendation, some ceremony of undeserved
recognition that Nitti had promoted for himself.
Then I had supposed it to be a formality, a Welcome, Sinner, to the True Path, where the only
penance to be done was the admission of prior
guilt. Finally I had realized that it was more than
that—but still underestimated the denouement.

HAROLD PRODKINS, NEPOTISTIC OFFICIAL
FROM EARTH, BELIEVED HIMSELF TO BE THE
SYMBOL OF COURAGE . . . SUCH CONDUCT VI-
OLATES THE CODES OF INTERSPECIES MO-
RALITY . . . WE HONOR NEITHER HIS INTENT
NOR HIS METHOD . . . WRONGED INDIVIDU-
ALS MAY FORGIVE OR REFUSE TO FORGIVE.
. . . YOU HAVE JUST WITNESSED THE MERCY-
KILLING OF HAROLD PRODKINS . . . JUSTICE
HAS BEEN DONE.

I heard it all, heard it all, in my mind's ear.

~~~~~~~ **Chapter 13** ~~~~~~~

Sᴌɪᴍ, graceful, the gossamer-winged creature took my hand. Was it male or female? Could its species be evolutionary cousins to Qumax's own? Incredible . . . yet, with those tentacles and antennae, not beyond the bounds of possibility.

I saw that others of its kind had alighted outside the ship. They waited for us.

Qumax said: "We are going to my Swarm Tyrant. We will be carried there by wing-power."

I was drawn with the others out into the open. Three baglike litters lay ready. Qumax got into the largest; Nancy and I into the two lesser ones.

Our litters were gently raised around the edges. Wings beat. A downdraft of air washed against the vegetation of the park. We were borne upward.

I peered cautiously down at the level streets and the pedestrians. I did not want to lose my balance or disturb the flight in any way, lest my hammock spin over and send me crashing down. Then I looked overhead at the wonderful pink-silver, silver-pink flash that were the great wings abeat in mild sunlight. None of it seemed strange, none really frightening. It was as though I had been on similar flights over similar cities in a life and time long forgotten.

I threw a thought at Qumax. *What are our litterbearers?*

Cops.

Police? Shades of Warden Nitti! *From what planet?*

Jamborango, naturally.

I lay back in the comfortably padded litter, reflecting that I had been right for once. Qumax's people were related to these others, if only in the sense that all life on a single planet had to be related. It was gratifying to see my perceptiveness rewarded occasionally.

Minutes later I became aware that we were climbing steadily higher. The buildings seemed endlessly tall, and there was a fragile beauty about them—like the spunglass towers and turrets and interconnecting walkways of some child's imaginative wonderland. I marveled that the members of any species here could live and grow up—really grow up—into hard, mean, cynically ruthless adults. Perhaps in a sense the natives here never had.

We passed over the last of the city and flew above a field of forty-foot-high Earth-sky-blue flowers with blossoms so big that a full grown man might walk inside with room to spare. They might even make decent houses, I thought dreamily. I watched the winged Jams going in and out of the big blue bells with what appeared to be harvesting baskets.

That must be our destination, Nancy thought. *There on the hill.*

I looked up the side of the small mountain that was thickly terraced with more of the giant blue

plants. There was a castle on the crest, or what
seemed like one. Walls of smoky-azure filled with
endlessly moving pink and silver lines; roof of spark-
ling amethyst; windows of a bright ocher and
saffron. Where the castle on the Strumbermians'
world had been all-dark, this one was all-light.
The other had been pungent nightmare; this was
sugared daydream. But each, unfortunately, was
too much: too much poignancy dulled the taste,
and too much sugar was sickening.

We ascended the hill and dipped over the castle.
We circled, traced rings in the sky, and finally
sailed in through a casement. We landed and were
let off in a room curtained round with liquidescent
silver drapes. The police escort departed with a
rush of wings. We were alone, with only a giant-
sized backless chair confronting us.

"Qumax—" I began.

Shhhhhhh-hh-h! the worm thought at me, as
though I had broken wind during a prayer. *HE is
about to give us an audience.*

He was really apprehensive. *But what about?* I
wanted to know.

He didn't answer. Through the drapes at the
back of the room flowed an unusually large Jamborang. This Jam's wings were deeper hued than
the others I had seen. His bearing was confident,
proud. There was a manner about him that was
decidedly different. A quality I could only think of
as intense masculinity.

Qumax's Swarm Tyrant moved to the throne.
He fluffed his wings back, formed a sleek bodily
arch and settled into the throne. His head turned.
Bright, all-seeing eyes stabbed at Qumax, Nancy,
me. The eyes rested. The Great One spoke, using the
language I had grown up with.

"Harold Prodkins, Minister of the Planet Earth's

nonexistent Inner-Galactic World Affairs—you have
a mission that the President of your world may or
may not choose to recognize as official, depending
on expedience. I know these things because my
errant offspring has communicated them, together
with your language. I have not, naturally, read
your mind."

"Yes, Swarm Tyrant," I said. Suddenly my bold
plan to wrest an apology from this creature seemed
rather foolish.

"You may address me as Qubuc. I am normally
referred to as the Qu Swarms' Tyrant, but Qubuc
has connotations in your language that you may
someday find entertaining. I am in a sense the
head buck."

"I find that amusing right now, Qubuc," I said.
Why did the great always inflate the value of their
droll humor?

"Harold Prodkins, your avowed mission had to
do with Qumax's unscheduled visit to your planet
and his behavior while staying there. You desire—I
believe 'demand' was your actual term—to have
official apology from the Jamborang government.
You feel that the Jamborangs should make good
on all damages as a matter of principle, and that
Qumax's Swarm Tyrant should be reprimanded.
Have I stated your case, Minister?"

I was sure he had been peeking into my mind.
Then I realized that had he done so, he would have
picked up my extreme present uncertainty and
known that he needed to make no concessions. I
swallowed. "You have, Qubuc."

The Swarm Tyrant twined his tentacles together.
"I have taken this matter up with the representatives of the Jamborang government, of which I am
one. It has been agreed unanimously that you do
have justice in your claim. An official apology will

be made to the Earth government, demands for damages will be satisfied . . . and you should know that I, the vexed parent who momentarily reverted to the behavior of his larval stage, have already been justly and severely reprimanded."

My knees felt like overcooked noodles. Had the President of Earth walked in I would not have been more astonished. Nor more certain that there was a catch the size of the Grand Canyon involved.

"However," Qubuc continued, and I knew it was coming now, "it is only fair to point out that the way Earthians are treated henceforth will depend on whether the Minister of Earth's Inner-Galactic World Affairs proves himself to be as concerned with personal integrity as was Warden Nitti—an individual who, I understand, was not particularly enamored of such concepts prior to the Strumbermian crisis."

Yes, this was it. The Strumbermians had had their test for True Humanoidism, and the Jamborangs would now unveil their variant. Was I expected to go through the whole charade again?

Was there a choice?

Qubuc was waiting for me to reply. My first impulse was to ask for a lawyer, but I realized that this would hardly impress anybody with my confidence and competence.

"Do you mean I have to stand trial too?" I asked.

"There is no word in your language precisely analogous to the process we have in mind. 'Trial' does suggest part of it, however."

My mouth went dry. "When? How long do I have to wait before learning what you are planning for me?"

The Swarm Tyrant untwined his tentacles. "The issue remains unresolved without prejudice until the hearing. You are under no compulsion. You may invoke it whenever you wish. A year from now, two years, ten years—"

"Thirty years?" I hazarded.

"If you prefer."

"And what do I do in the meantime—rot in jail?"

"You will be a guest of the planet, with complete freedom of movement. Or you may choose to travel the galaxy. Since it was a Jamborangan national who precipitated your journey here, you will be entertained at our expense."

"For thirty years?" I still wasn't sure what I was fencing with.

"Jamborango can afford it."

"Suppose not at all? Suppose I get a ride back to Earth instead of signing up for this trial?"

"That is your privilege, naturally. But then the issue would be held in doubt. If Earthians do not have the courage to re-examine their own standards and conduct, they cannot petition for admittance to galactic affairs."

Yes, it was clear enough. More subtle, more sophisticated than the Strumbermian process, but essentially the same. I was hostage for my world. If I did not cooperate, Earth could be in serious trouble. But if I *did* cooperate, did I have even half the chance that I had had in gravbop?

"I protest," I said, far less confident than I hoped I sounded. "You're no better than the Strumbermians. If dealing with them was wrong, then so is dealing with you on this basis!"

"You misunderstand," Qubuc replied imperturbably. "We do not put you in any arena, even figuratively. We do not make any judgment concerning you. The charges are made by your own conscience. With the help of the Galactic Court you will decide for yourself whether you really did commit treason to your own species and betray a willful disregard for morality as you comprehend it. Your actions suggest that you gambled the welfare of your world in order to save your own life, Nancy Dilsmore's, and my son Qumax's."

"For saving your larva, I get blamed?"

"Not by me. But the legitimacy of the method must be ascertained to your own satisfaction."

Nancy spoke up. "But aren't there extenuating circumstances?"

"If there are," said Qubuc, "Harold Prodkins must consider them in making his judgment."

"Harold," Nancy said. "I don't like this." She took my hand and squeezed it. "Really, I don't think you should—"

But I knew that she, along with everyone else, here and home on Earth, would look down on me if I were to refuse. A man who submits willingly to evil—not that I had done so!—and then declines to examine his reasons isn't worthy of much respect. "Suppose I'm guilty," I said. "And I—atone. Will that make a difference in the way Earth is regarded?"

"Yes."

I shook my head. "If I'm tried, I probably get it in the neck. Explosively, on a galactic network. If I'm not tried, my world probably gets it."

"Harold, that isn't—"

"Shut up, Nancy." I wasn't sure whether I loved her or hated her. Had not been sure for some time, in fact.

"No," said Qubuc. "Your world will not be punished."

"Not directly, you mean. All that will happen is that Earth will be effectively prevented from becoming part of things, galaxywise. Earth will be like a small island surrounded by great nations— given subsistence aid if she begs prettily enough, or laughed at or ignored—but never helped or permitted to become powerful and civilized."

Qubuc did not answer. He did not need to.

"How soon can I have my trial?"

"Immediately, if you prefer."

"Sooner, if you please." Nothing like calling a bluff.

Qubuc slid a tentacle down his right chair-arm. "Sooner it will be, Harold Prodkins of Earth. Your presentation began when you entered this chamber."

Oops! Well, I had asked for it. The Tyrant had called *my* bluff. He was as sharp a politician as cousin Freddy, unsurprisingly. Of course when I specified sooner than immediately I was asking for retroactivity!

Drapes rippled with flashes of silver. Nancy, Qumax and I were abruptly surrounded by aliens.

"You may not be familiar with Galactic procedure," said Qubuc. "Our courts, whose jurors are selected by lot from all the civilized populations of the Galaxy, function merely as aids to the individual conscience. There is therefore very little of what you call due process. No prosecutor, no defending attorney, no real judging, other than by yourself. No traps or deceptions or evasions, no authority other than your own. The entities you see about you are experts in psychology, integrity and ethics. They are not present in person, but only by projected image, for they reside as far away as fifty thousand light years. They are here to assist you, Harold Prodkins—to help you decide for yourself."

"To brainwash me, you mean!"

"No, Harold Prodkins. Your conclusions will be freely formed and you will not be externally guided to them. The court's assistance will be only such as you yourself direct."

"I'll believe that when I experience it," I said.

I looked at the faces—flat faces, long faces, big faces, bug faces, smug faces, firm faces, worm faces. It was nice that they were there to *help* me: had they been my prosecutors I could not have stood it. "What do I do?"

"Think over what happened without a mind-block. Let your thoughts come out openly—uncontrived, without conscious attempt to conceal or justify. Be afraid of revealing nothing. There are machines and drugs that would aid you in this process, but unless you request them, we prefer. . . ."

"This is the Galactic Court? This is really my trial?"

From the assembled aliens there came one united, massive thought: *THE GALACTIC COURT IS NOW IN SESSION. HAROLD PRODKINS, EARTH'S OFFICIAL MINISTER OF INNER-GALACTIC WORLD AFFAIRS, IS CHARGED BY HIS OWN LOGIC WITH HIGH TREASON—TO BOTH HIS SPECIES AND THE GREATER WELFARE OF THE GALAXY.*

It was the Galactic Court, all right. Now I wished I'd waited a decade or three. I fastened my eyes on the huge, fat, remotely manlike alien that seemed to be nearest. He was checking a machine that looked suspiciously like a lie-detector. "I thought no machines," I said.

"Machines will be used to check fluctuations in your electrical pattern," Qubuc explained. "In this way it will be known whether you are being honest with yourself, without the intrusion of any other mind. The machines thus help preserve your privacy in these difficult deliberations—though it would be best for you to be completely open."

"Oh, hell," I said. "What chance have I got?"

"Just think through recent events—the area of

your life that troubles you," Qubuc advised. "The truth will emerge."

Like offal, I thought. The truth would kill me! But what else was there?

Rapidly, not giving myself a chance to think about the manner I was destroying myself, I opened my mind to the entire assemblage and thought back to the area that troubled me: the first time I had gravbopped.

I had been afraid of Crog. I had been confused, worried about attempting this violent sport. I had been fearful for the Strumbermian child Ogue, though obviously she meant nothing to me. But fear of being judged Non-Humanoid—that had been uppermost. Strange, for that concept didn't bother me now. Why had it been so important then?

Reluctantly I had agreed to play ... and I had played reluctantly until Ogue taught me that I could be killed that way. Somehow I had been convinced that it would be planetary disaster for the human species to be labeled Non-True-Humanoid. Therefore what I was doing was pro-survival for my world. I had fought bitterly and hard ... and I had won the first match.

I still did not like what I had done to Ogue; that bothered me, of course. But at the time I had had no choice. How could I be blamed, when I had protested more than once having to fight Ogue, but been overruled?

But then, having defeated the Strumbermian child, I had found myself recognized as a True Humanoid. I knew then that if I defeated Crog I would not only secure my own release from the Strumbermian stronghold, but would also establish Earth's independence and respectability. It was, I'd thought, a slick way of doing things.

I stopped thinking, feeling morally justified. The

problem was not so fraught with guilt after all. True, I could have been more gentle with the child Ogue—but that was hard to do in the heat of battle. I was certain that I had exonerated myself.

Nothing happened. There were no thoughts of approval from the aliens. No expressions on their vastly varied faces. Merely an oppressive mental silence.

Well, what more do you want? I was feeling self-righteous and indignant.

A character who looked like a dark blue warthog put a bilious green finger to the side of his bristly gray snout. Small eyes, murderously red, stared from the monster-mask. *Why, Harold Prodkins? Are you your species' keeper?* I don't know how I knew he was the one communicating, but I knew.

"Of course not!" I exclaimed. And paused. It was as though I heard Cain making the same denial to God. And if I were *not* my species' keeper, who had appointed me to decide Earth's fate?

The warthog waited, and the court with him, and Nancy and Qumax too.

Who *had* appointed me to make any representations on behalf of Earth? Why was it up to *me* to decide the fate of humanity?

I had an answer for that: my cousin Freddy, President of Earth, had appointed me. My mission was Official, even though Freddy had tried to coop me up in Lucifernia to make sure I wouldn't bungle it.

I stopped thinking, again feeling morally justified. There was no doubt my audience would see the perfect case I had established.

Were you obligated to gravbop? thought an apple-cheeked cockatrice.

Well, naturally! I'd had no choice. If I was not a True Humanoid, by Strumbermian definitions,

Earth would be invaded. I would have been mind-probed, then probably killed along with Nancy and Qumax, and Earth would have been invaded. I had had to fight—to gravbop—to save the lives of those dear to me and to preserve my world.

The court waited noncommittally. Evidently they did not feel it was over yet. What did they want?

The lie-detector-operator thought: *That is not the whole truth, Harold Prodkins. Your body is tense and afraid.*

But I had clarified everything! What trick was this?

Silence.

Of course there *had* been that cruelty to Ogue. Once I had her down, I shouldn't have brained her again, at least not so hard. But I had been under stress, and in a violent mood; I had kicked at rats and despised bugs.

In fact, I hadn't thought so much of worms either. Or Earthian females. Strange. But irrelevant. I had done what I had to do.

So why was my body so tight I could hardly breathe?

"Harold, tell them about the interrogation," Nancy said.

I looked at her, blue-eyed and desirable. I knew then that I had loved her; that I still loved her even though I had lusted after the—

Irrelevant.

"That doesn't concern this court," I said.

"Yes it does!" She opened her mind to the court: *Harold Prodkins was interrogated privately by the Strumbermians aboard their raider. Something happened to him during that interview. Something I don't understand. After that he was somehow changed.*

"Nancy, stop that!" I cried, furiously embarrassed. I tried to grab her shoulders, to shake her out of it before she destroyed my case. She executed a skillful half-twist and I had to drop to my knees to avoid being thrown into the image of a pulsing jellyfish.

Galactic Court, make Harold Prodkins reveal what happened during the interrogation—for there, if anywhere, you find the extenuating circumstances.

"Extenuating circumstances! You idiot blonde, I've already won my case!"

"You've lost it," she said simply.

The court waited. And then I knew that I *had* lost. They did not buy my reasoning about the gravbop contests.

We can force you to look at yourself, thought a black alien with blue eyes that seemed like starholes. It was a kindly offer, not a threat. But I did not want to be forced into anything.

"I'll help you, Harold," Nancy said. She took my hand, held it, and looked earnestly at me. It was as though a lot of things had never been. . . .

Vividly I recalled how I had felt when the Strumbermians had come for me. I had been scared, both for myself and for the others. But more than that, I had been determined to prove myself—to myself. If Qumax could do it, why not I?

Crog had offered me scrotch. I had glugged it, not out of camaraderie but out of need. And after I had glugged—so eager, so defiant, and yet with so much acquiescence—I had discovered the Earthians and Strumbermians were really brother species.

Mind whirling—knowing things I had always known, yet knowing them with far more immediacy—I had followed Flu into the adjoining stateroom. To a waiting pallet, and then—

I cut off that thought. I did not like standing naked before this entire alien court.

Tears brimmed Nancy's eyes. "Oh, Harold, I'm

so sorry for you," she said. "It must have been terrible!"

I swallowed and looked past her at the blue warthog. How could I tell her that it *hadn't* been terrible? I was disgusted now, but then—well, Nancy had to be aware of the nature of that experience.

The warthog had his eyes shut. All the aliens had their optics turned off.

"They are conferring," said Qubuc. "The jury is out, as you might put it, though it is you and not they who constitute the jury. Soon they will return—to aid you in fathoming the truth and in deciding your sentencing."

I now appreciated why Nitti had wanted to die.

Eyes popped open. The blue warthog thought at me:

Harold Prodkins, there are circumstances under which even the most civilized of beings is not considered responsible for its own thoughts and actions. It is our advisory opinion that such is the present case.

"But—" I had swung from confidence in my exoneration to a complete acceptance of guilt. Prunians!

Let me explain, thought a purple chipmunk. *All highly evolved creatures have minds consisting in part of a conscious, a subconscious and an id—or a top-mind, middle-mind and instinctive mind that holds the energies of your most primitive forebears. The Strumbermians are subcivilized because they lack the means to control this basic energy-source, the id. They lack, properly speaking, a conscience. To them, instinctive behavior is by definition rational behavior. Scrotch dulls the conscience of a normal humanoid—paralyzes it to such an extent that the id is without control. To us, a humanoid in such condition is maimed. To a Strumbermian, this is the state of the True Humanoid.*

Ouch! I thought back, reassessing. I had evaluated Nancy by Prunian standards—and found her far less blatant, and therefore wanting. I had examined the gravbop contests from a politician's position of expedience with hardly an apology to the ethics involved. I might ordinarily have gravbopped, but hardly with my world at stake.

Do you understand about the Prunians? thought the jellyfish.

I shivered. I did not want *that* subject explored in public detail!

Prunians are skilled psychiatric workers, from the Strumbermian view. Other species regard them as interspecies prostitutes. While you were under the influence of scrotch, they suggested a view of reality that would make your id-directed urges acceptable. The Strumbermians' purpose demanded that your thinking be changed, but not so much that their tampering would be evident to you.

Suddenly I saw that my primary motive—the protection of my home world from invasion—had been spurious. Why should hard-pressed Strumbermians undertake such an expensive project, when what they wanted was allies? They had used that empty threat to prod me into committing Earth to their cause—and my scrotch-addled brain had not cried foul.

"I really am innocent, then?" I asked, hardly daring to believe it. "Innocent of whatever I thought I was guilty of?"

That is for you to decide, an alien thought gently.

"You now have sufficient knowledge to make your decision, Harold Prodkins," Qubuc said. "You may want to consider the matter for some time. Your hearing before this friendly witnessing and advisory body is over, since the truth has been brought out. That is the only purpose of such a session—to establish the truth. The *meaning* of the truth is your own concern." The alien court faded and the silver curtains fell back.

"That—that's what Nitti went through?"

"Yes."

"And he decided to—"

Nancy grabbed my arm. "But not you, Harold! He didn't have scrotch for an excuse. You'll find yourself innocent if I have to—well, I will anyway!"

And she kissed me once, and I know I would never suicide as long as she was near.

~~~~~~~~ **Chapter 14** ~~~~~~~~

"**N**ow," Nancy remarked as we settled down to informal chat with Qumax and his Swarm Tyrant, "I have to see about that corcos Lamorcos contract."

"Nancy!" I cried, remembering what I had learned about galactic slavery. "You didn't sign up with the Spevarian—?"

"No, of course not," she said, and I sank back, relieved. "We were interrupted by the Strumbermian raid on the ship. And I wanted to discuss it with you. So I've asked Bumvelde to come here—"

"Ridiculous!" Qumax said.

"By no means," Qubuc corrected him. Then, to Nancy: "Do you wish to complete the contract? You would sacrifice certain personal rights, and would have to leave for Spevar instead of returning to Earth with your Minister Prodkins."

"You're not seriously considering—" I began, amazed. But I saw that she was.

"I was greatly impressed with what I learned about Spevarians and galactic civilization," she said. "My research appetite was whetted. A chance to experience life on Spevar in the service of a recognized Spevarian Scholar—what extraterrestrialogist wouldn't jump at the chance?"

"Nancy, there's no question of your going through with this," I protested. "You're a bright lass and you know you'd be sacrificing your freedom. Think of it, Nancy—slavery!"

"Knowledge," she said. "More knowledge than we of Earth could otherwise dream of gaining."

"In *slavery?* Nancy, you must be mad!"

"Harold, what we think of as slavery isn't—"

"*Is* slavery! Don't give me that, wench! I know a thing or two, too, you know. So for some systems it isn't slavery, it's just the ownership of individuals by other individuals. That's really doubletalk—the kind some Earth societies have been famous for!"

"Harold, how can you imagine anything so stupid? This *isn't* Earth."

"I know what it is, Nancy. Do you? My conscience is in control now—what happened to yours? I suppose if you'd been offered an excellent contract as a courtesan you'd have jumped at it!"

"HAROLD!" Color rose to her face and I knew that it was not going to be male-logic that would dominate. "Harold, you're beneath contempt when you talk that way!"

"Neither slavery nor prostitution are considered to be dishonorable trades in the galaxy," Qubuc observed.

"You don't know these Earthians, Tyrant," Qumax said, frying. He was still as bratty as ever.

At that point seal-like Bumvelde arrived.

"Corcos Lamorcos!" Nancy cried. "I agree to your contract. I want to leave for Spevar, not to return to Earth again. I don't think I ever want to see this—this *gravbopper* again!"

My head whirled, as it had so often in the past few days. I knew I had to stop her, yet I didn't see how I could. She was, as the saying went, free, white and eighteen, and I had no hold over her.

"Perhaps, Harold Prodkins," Qubuc said gently, "you would care to go along with her? You are welcome to remain here, but I'm sure you could also get a Spevarian contract."

"Thanks for nothing," I said diplomatically. *You're seriously suggesting that I double the error by becoming a slave myself?*

"I don't think you'd regret a contract, Harold Prodkins. If this imperious female means as much to you as appears . . ."

I considered it. I certainly didn't want to sacrifice the very independence I'd struggled so hard to preserve for myself and my world (rightly or wrongly), but with Nancy so difficult . . .

"It would not last forever, and then you could warn other Earthians about such contracts—assuming you'd be disappointed, of course."

Hmmmm, now that he put it that way. . . .

Yes, by golly! Nancy was worth it.

"Bumvelde," I said, "I demand to be your slave!"

The Spevarian thought a blob of astonishment at me.

"If Nancy Dilsmore enters your service, then I insist on the right to enter also. It is my duty to Earth to find out about corcos Lamorcos contracts."

"Impossible. My contractees must be content if they are to prove worth the investment. Nancy Dilsmore wishes not to see you again."

"But—"

"Definitely not. Only if she should give her approval."

"Nancy—" I said, baffled.

"Harold!" Her eyes were luminous. "You'd become a slave? For me?"

"I already am a slave to you."

"Why Harold—that's, that's—"

"Stupid? Foolish? Idiotic? Romantic? Sure, all those things, but—"

"Ohhh, Harold—could you, will you—I mean, why don't you ask me?"

"Huh?" I could have used a glug of scrotch to clarify things.

"Marriage, you stupid foolish idiotic romantic! That's what you had in mind, isn't it?"

"Why, ah, sure," I said, terrified.

"Then we might as well have the ceremony now, don't you think?"

"I guess." I felt stupidfoolishidioticromantic.

Nancy said a few words to Bumvelde, or maybe she thought some thoughts.

"Certainly," the Spevarian said. Rapidly he ran over the terms of a standard five-year corcos Lamorcos contract for one mated unit consisting of two sexes. With our minds only half on corcos Lamorcos, Nancy and I agreed and the two Jamborangs served as witnesses for the completed contract. Bumvelde announced that his contractees would be allowed several long Jamborango days as Qubuc's castle-guests; at the end of that period the Spevarian would come for us. It was, we were given to understand, the equivalent of an enlistment bonus, or an Earthly honeymoon.

When the agreements were complete, Qubuc drew the curtains again and the entire Galactic Court reappeared. A beautiful sky-blue octopus moved to the front of the panoramic image. Nancy and I joined hands and bowed our heads reverently before it. There was a brief exchange of alien thoughts, some private, some open. Things settled down to a very respectful silence. Then the octopus thought at us:

CIVILIZED BEINGS, INTELLIGENT ENTITIES ... PEOPLE ALL: WE ARE GATHERED TOGETHER IN THIS IMAGE AT THIS TIME TO WITNESS THE OFFICIAL REGISTERING OF TWO INDIVIDUALS OF THE SAME SPECIES—EARTHIANS HAROLD PRODKINS AND NANCY DILSMORE—AS MATES. BY THE SUPREME ALL-PERVADING INTELLIGENCE, BY THE UNIVERSAL GOODNESS, BY THE TIMELESS NEVER-ENDING SEA OF STARS—

By the time he had finished, I had never felt more officially anything in my life. I squeezed Nancy's hand and I knew without receiving her thoughts that she felt the same way about it. Bumvelde promised to show up in person in a few days, the Galactic Court vanished again, and Nancy and I were alone in a palace of silver drapes with Qumax and Qubuc.

Later, but not much later, alone in our highly private room, Nancy and I learned the full extent of what telepathy could do for us. Baggie-dresses and prudery were crippling limitations rather than assurers of innocence; before the dawn, we were rid of both limitations and innocence to an extent that few Earth-born humans could be.

And you know, Prunians were like cows in comparison.

Common sense tells me that Nancy and I could not have honeymooned on any world quite so wonderful. Yet we did. We spent the equivalent of many Earth days sightseeing, carried by winged members of the Qu Swarm; we visited the harvesting fields and entered one of the big blossoms in the company of Qubuc; we scaled mountains and

visited the capital with Qumax; swam in a spark-
ling, rose-scented sea; lazed beneath a sun of just
the right warmth and no burning; loved, constantly
and in many ways, none solely physical. During all
this time only one flaw kept away complete happi-
ness: the dreadful knowledge that my wife and I
were soon to be taken into slavery.

Nancy explained over and over that slavery, to
the galactics, was not really onerous. She drew
educated parallels between the galactic institution
and the ideal Earth had never achieved.

I only pretended to follow. So maybe it was no
worse than the buying and selling of baseball and
football players. No matter how benevolent the
owner, I was not about to be the completely willing slave of anyone.

Then Bumvelde arrived. He had left his wives
and children on Spevar and come to take us home.
Much to my discomfiture, I found him to be every
inch the alien gentleman. So cultured was he and
so widely respected that Qubuc insisted that he
stay a few days as castle-guest himself. They were
to discuss the sort of things that Qubuc enjoyed
discussing, and Nancy and I could take the opportunity to get to know our new master gradually.

And we did—for days. The second day Nancy,
Bumvelde and I went to the bottom of a glassy sea
in a transparent submarine. We maneuvered it
about and watched the strange, colorful sea-crea-
tures that human minds had never imagined. I
took over the controls ... and it came to me,
insanely as such a thought will come, that with a
bit of maneuvering I might readily destroy this
fragile creature. Bumvelde was probably an excellent swimmer, if his seal-like appearance meant
anything, but there were other ways. . . .

The moment passed. I maneuvered us safely past

the jagged coral, through an underwater cave and
out into the undersea light. I surfaced us, brought
us into dock. Despite everything, I was glad I hadn't
done anything rash. That would have been the
Strumbermian way.

As we approached the tie-up, I saw the circling
figure of a flyer. We bumped to rest and the flyer
landed, folded wings and stood waiting for us. I
put the hatch-cover up, looked out and recognized
it as one of the Qu Swarm. The differences between swarms were subtle, but I was getting adept
at noting them.

"News," sang the flyer. "Prince Qumax now enters the cocoon."

"Now?" I repeated stupidly.

The flyer's wings flopped. "At this very moment.
Hurry, so that you may visit with him."

It was like birth, I thought—this quick, all-but-
unexpected process that was to make of Qumax a
strong, sensible adult. A cocoon, and from it would
emerge—what? I couldn't quite imagine this im-
pudent brat as a noble-browed, fully-winged Qubuc.
Yet such a transformation, we had been assured,
could and would take place. Qumax the larva to
Qumax the adult, wings and all. Incredible!

We landed in our litter in record time on the
castle's grounds and were escorted immediately
inside by excited though carefully respectful flyers.
Through a tall door, down a long hall and into a
large room in which Qumax hung head-down from
a high, ornate rafter. The gray silk-sack now en-
closed two-thirds of his body. His head went round
and round, suggesting that he was a caterpillar
and not a cabbage worm. His dark, overly intelligent eyes were shut. There was a look on his face
that spoke of needs and pleasures more ancient

and complete than the tribe of Man would ever know.

We stood and watched. After a while it began to seem a bore. Waiting in a maternity hospital was like this, I had been told.

"Uh—how many children do you have?" I asked Qubuc.

He was rapt. "A full four hundred and one, by your reckoning. Qumax is the one. Some swarms never receive the Prince—the one capable of founding his own swarm. But my fortunate two hundred wives and I, we fulfilled our quota of neuters and females and—"

"You mean to say that these things are regulated?"

"They must be, unfortunately."

"But—isn't that a little cruel? I mean—neuters?"

"Not for the individuals involved, Harold Prodkins. In many ways, the neuters have all the best of it. It's the neuters who do all the big important things while the males and females are bound to their planet and their swarm. I confess that I sympathize with Qumax's desire to escape and live as an adventurer. I had the same urge when I was a larva. Sometimes, even today, I would almost trade all my beloved wives and my position in the government to be a traveling author, a vagabond entertainer or even a simple police Jam. But we are as we are and those of us who are destined to rule a swarm have our lives and careers set from the moment of conception."

"Hmmmm, yes, I can see that such a large swarm might cramp an entity's style a bit. Still, I'd think that it's really the Tyrants who are controlling things. Don't you agree with me, Qubuc?"

"No, I'm afraid not. A policeJam who saves lives and prevents disasters, a ship's captain who is responsible for the security of his vessel, a much-

traveled author who really adds to our understanding of the people of the universe—these are all
more important than I. But I—now that I look at
Qumax, I confess that I feel rather important."

His words brought back my attention to the
fast-disappearing cocooned head. Suddenly it
thought at us:

*Harold, Nancy, Bumvelde (you slavemaster!)—I
wish all of you present at my Maturity Flight.*

"Maturity Flight—when's that?" I asked. I was
afraid we'd have to leave for Spevar before that
date.

*Not long as the galaxy measures time, Harold
Prodkins. Only long enough for you to get to appreciate your wife. It will be a span of time roughly
equivalent to fourteen of your Earth-years. . . .*

Chapter 15

SOME of the most momentous days in our lives begin the most slowly. Take for instance that morning on Spevar, thirteen and a half Earth-years after Nancy and I had last seen Qumax. . . .

It was one of those frequent contracted holidays. This meant that today Nancy did not assist Bumvelde in his historical research and that I did not demonstrate Prodkins' Solar Pool Tables at Bumvelde's factory. Otherwise all was normal. We were out on our acres-wide, self-regulating lawn in front of our "slave-mansion"—a careful antebellum reconstruction built to my very specific order. The day was typically, Spevarianly, perfect. Nancy had brought out an armload of books and periodicals, plus letters and other bits of mail. She dropped these on the ground underneath the spreading branches of an oak tree—one of three we had imported as seedlings—and stood frowning pensively. Nancy, it seemed, was always frowning pensively. It made her very attractive.

"Sometimes," she said, "I could wish that Earth had never made its debut."

I smiled. "That didn't used to be your story."

"Yours either, you ungrammatical lout."

I let her drop the mail beside me, then reached up and attempted to pull her down beside me. She struggled only a little—no karate chops—and then gave up. There was not, I was sure, much else she had to do today. "Nancy," I said, "do you realize that we have now been here the equivalent of thirteen and a half of our Earth-years?"

"I realize it very well," she said.

"But—we haven't aged. Not noticeably, anyway. You've still got a figure like a—"

"Harold!" But the protest was the reflex of over a decade. She had not worn a baggie in all that time. "It must be the air," she said after a bit. "It's always like spring here. I feel almost as though I could expect to reach a thousand—Earth-years."

"Why not Spevarian?" I asked. "They're approximately twelve times as long."

She sighed and leaned her head on my shoulder. "Harold, have you thought-checked Bumqu this morning?"

"Not this morning," I said. "The kid's nearly twelve—"

"Thirteen."

"Nearly thirteen, then. He doesn't want his old man checking on him all the time. That's the trouble with most mothers—they don't let their sons mature naturally. I'll bet he's off somewhere with Bumvelde's kids, planning a new space-scooter or something. What are all those letters—more paperwork?"

"More orders for Prodkins 'S-P Tables. I do believe you'll even be getting orders from Earth soon."

"Wouldn't doubt it," I said. "There are still people on Earth just stupid enough to pay a premium just because a table is manufactured here instead of on the planet where the fool game originated. Funny how I was so worried about the corcos Lamorcos contract, wasn't it?"

"Funny now, perhaps. The most trying thing was the way I couldn't convince you. I knew what the contract was, but you refused to believe me. It's a diabolical arrangement, really. Spevarians such as Bumvelde travel about and gain control of individuals new to the galactic scene by the one temporary contract. It's like striking gold—"

"Striking oil. You *find* gold."

"For a gold-strike? Without your knowledge of the Solar Pool game, he never would have gotten anywhere building a factory."

"But without his funds and knowledge, I couldn't have done anything with that knowledge. And speaking of knowledge, what about all the learning of an Earthian extraterrestrialogist he acquired in the bargain?"

"But think of how much knowledge the extraterrestrialogist accumulated," she said. "Those books and thought-recordings are doing very well on Earth—almost as well as Bumvelde's own monographs on Earth-culture are doing nearer the center of the Galaxy."

"It's a good deal all the way around," I agreed. "Except of course for competitors. Contractees get security and a chance to really profit and build in a more advanced society. Contractors get the fresh ideas and insights."

I looked at the top envelope of the mail she had brought. It was addressed to Galactic Ambassador Harold W. Prodkins—an unofficial title that had been conferred on me along with the official recognition of my mission to Jamborango. "In undertaking to write the definitive biography of your late cousin, Frederik Michael Bascum. . . ."

"Good God," I said, "another one!" That made several hundred definitive biographies of a man who deserved at most a historical footnote. I could understand Earth's interest in the former president, but when it came to the way he was idolized I was often tempted to give the true story.

Fortunately there were other books heralding the great individuals responsible for the great changes that had been made. There was one on Karlos Nitti (so *that* was the warden's first name!) that, fictive as it was, still resulted in badly needed prison reform. And there had been the runaway best seller *For God and Qumax*, purporting to give the full story of the worm's visit to Earth. Yes, there had been plenty of entertaining fiction!

"Here's what we've been waiting for," Nancy said.

I looked at her in surprise. She was holding up an engraved card. "An official invitation to Qumax's Maturity Flight," she said.

I grabbed the card away from her. At the bottom was a small table converting local Spevarian time to Jamborango capital time. I looked at the postmark and saw that the card had been delayed in the spacemail.

"Good God," I said. "That thing is for tomorrow. Bumvelde will be along any minute to pick us up."

Bumvelde, his two wives and six younger children, Bumqu, Nancy and I made about seven kids too many on the Spevarian's space yacht. Bumvelde piloted us down through the atmosphere, and all the noise inside was beyond belief.

"Pop! Hey, Pop!"

I turned in my seat and faced my offspring—
plumpish, round-faced and freckled. "What is it,
son?"

"Do I have to wear this—this—"

"That's a fine wool suit, son. It's what they wear
on Earth for formal occasions. Anything more comfortable would be an insult to our host's Maturity
Flight!"

"Aw, who cares about a Jam's binge?"

"I do, son. And your mother also."

"Awwww."

"And you needn't look as though it's a discrimi-
natory torture I'm putting you through. I've got on
a suit just as well-made and just as scratchy."

"Harolde and Nande don't! None of the other
kids do!"

"Different cultures, different customs. You must
remember that your people are from Earth and
that Earthians have never been entirely logical."

"Huh, especially parents." I watched my son
lean back with a magazine, STRUMBERMIAN
TERROR TALES, and I closed my eyes. I thought
of all the changes on Earth and wondered if I'd
ever go there again—to visit, since no one in his
right mind would want to live on such a planet.
Things were better now—much better. Our prisoner-
coveralls had changed the styles back home, and a
lot of other changes had followed. Artificial prudery was gone, and morals had not been noticeably
degraded by its absence. As a matter of fact, it
might be true that Earthians today were both more
moral and more sensible (the two qualities not
being synonymous) than they had ever been prior
to Galactic contact.

"Pop?"

"What now, Bumqu?"

"Is it true what it says in this magazine, Pop? Is this Qumax Jam really getting this super-fast star-yacht as a present?"

Startled, I looked at the magazine. It was a different one; evidently he had tired of Strum atrocities and gone on to a Galactic-gossip publication. A picture showed a long racy hull that scintillated against a background of stars. It would hold a very large harem, I thought, and wondered again how sheiks and Tyrants managed honeymoons. I imagined it would make any male either a tyrant or a cringing sissy in short order.

"Pop?"

"Huh? Oh, it's true—perfectly true. It says here you'll get to go through it, along with all the other guests."

"That's good," said Bumqu.

Things change slowly on Jamborango—so slowly that thirteen and one half Earth-years appeared to have slipped away unnoticed. The streets were still flowing silver and the pedestrians still came in as bewildering a variety. Winged Jamborangs flew us from the busy spaceport to Qubuc's castle; here we mingled with the crowds that covered half the mountainside, visited the fabulous starship whose maiden voyage would really be what we would call a mass honeymoon and the Jams called Maturity Flight. We renewed, as the saying goes, old acquaintances.

"Up there," Captain Fuzzpuff, once of the *Comet's Tail*, said, pointing a top right hand, "you see the doorway where they'll come out: two hundred carefully picked maiden worms and your old friend Qumax."

I strained my eyes but could see nothing other

than pink and silver lines on the castle's smoky blue background. "You Pmpermians have better eyes than we Earthians."

I see it! I see it! thought one of Bumvelde's litter. Harold, probably.

No you don't! No you don't! another—Nande? challenged.

"Harold," Nancy said with annoyance, "I can't see Bumqu anywhere."

"He'll show up."

"I lost Harold, too," complained one of Bumvelde's wives.

So I had misguessed, again, in identifying those little seals. "Don't worry," I said, "they'll—"

"Mom! Mom!"

"Why, Nande, what is it? Why have you been running so hard?"

"It's the boys, Mom. They said they were going to steal a ride on the Jam starship."

"WHAT!"

"And the others got scared. But Bumqu said he'd go even if the others *were*—what kind of animal is a 'chicken,' Mom? So he slipped inside and when nobody was watching, he hid inside a cabinet. The other boys waited for a while and then one of them said Bumqu must've smothered—"

"Oh, no!" Nancy cried.

"—but he hadn't because when they tapped on the door he answered. Then he said the door was locked and he couldn't get out and he's spilt some sort of itchy powder all over him. Then he said, 'Go away!' And—"

"That boy! I'll skin him alive!" I said.

"That won't be necessary!" a strange deep voice boomed.

I whirled. Half lying, half hovering on iridescent wings, was the biggest, most masculinely beautiful Jam I'd ever seen. In his large tentacle, close to his broad bright chest, he held the scaredest-looking freckle-faced going-on-thirteen-year-old Earthboy imaginable.

"There's one of us in every generation," said the adult Qumax.

THE DRAGON REBORN

Sequel to *The Great Hunt*

Book Three
~~of~~
The Wheel of Time

by

Robert Jordan

Praise for *Eye of the World*

"A powerful vision of good and evil...fascinating people moving through a rich and interesting world." —*Orson Scott Card*

"Richly detailed...fully realized, complex adventure."
—*Library Journal*

"A combination of Robin Hood and Stephen King that is hard to resist...Jordan makes the reader care about these characters as though they were old friends." —*Milwaukee Sentinel*

Praise for *The Great Hunt*

"Jordan can spin as rich a world and as event-filled a tale as [Tolkien]...will not be easy to put down." —*ALA Booklist*

"Worth re-reading a time or two." —*Locus*

"This is good stuff...Splendidly characterized and cleverly plotted...The Great Hunt is a good book which will always be a good book. I shall certainly [line up] for the third volume."
—*Interzone*

The Dragon Reborn
coming in hardcover in August, 1991